ALL THE VISIONS

Rudy Rucker

Transreal Books

Paperback ISBN: 978-1-940948-01-0
Ebook ISBN: 978-1-940948-02-7
Hardback ISBN: 978-1-940948-03-4

The cover painting, *All the Visions*, is
by Rudy Rucker. The author photo
was taken by David Abrams.

This is the second edition of *All the Visions*.
The first edition was published in 1991 by Ocean
View Books, Denver CO, bound with *Space Baltic*,
a collection of Anselm Hollo's poems.

Transreal Books
Los Gatos, California
www.transrealbooks.com

For Caldwell, Hank, Ace, Hondo, Anselm…
And always Audrey

Contents

Preface

I wrote *All the Visions* when I was still using a typewriter—typing it in bursts between June 21 and July 8, 1983. I was thirty-seven, and living as a freelance writer in Lynchburg, Virginia. The book is a memory dump of tales about my quest for enlightenment. But the characters have made-up names. I meant for *All the Visions* to be a beatnik novel.

My inspiration was Jack Kerouac's *On the Road*. To mimic the master, I wrote *All the Visions* on a single long roll of paper. I rigged up the roll on a length of broomstick propped up behind my good old rose-red IBM Selectric typewriter. *All the Visions* was about eighty feet long when I was done.

I improvised most of *All the Visions*, but in a few spots I typed in copies of things I'd written before, such as some short memory sketches, excerpts from my high-school journals, a vision from my novel *Spacetime Donuts*, and some poems of mine. The poems appeared in my early chapbook, *Light Fuse and Get Away*, and in my *Transreal!* anthology. I also typed in a story about a wild day in New York City with my friend Eddie Marritz—the original version of this piece later appeared as "Drugs and Live Sex—NYC 1980" in the long-forgotten *Journal Wired*.

In order to emphasize the book's scrolly origins, I initially formatted it into three very long paragraphs. But in this second edition, I've put in more paragraph breaks, adding them at spots where I might have paused to catch my breath—like a horn-man resting between choruses, as Jack K. would say. In order to indicate my original just-three-paragraphs formatting, I've sectioned the text into three numbered "takes."

I've also revised *All the Visions* in other ways—tweaking the prose, clarifying the meanings, making some cuts, rearranging blocks of text, and adding a few extra scenes. At first I felt uneasy about making edits, but I feel the second edition is more novelistic, and closer to my original intentions. And of course Jack revised his single-paragraph *On the Road* scroll numerous times between its origins in April, 1951, and its eventual publication in 1957.

Although the narrator of *All the Visions* is passionately interested in math, literature, mysticism, and his family, these concerns are overshadowed by his monomaniacal focus on getting high. In 1983, and for another decade or so after that, I thought it was cool and funny to write this way. I wanted to seem *bad*. I didn't see my characters' binges and freak-outs as sad or painful—I thought of them as bold expeditions into the unknown.

By now I've long since changed my way of life, but I still find *All the Visions* to be an entertaining beatnik riff, a type of book that I've always enjoyed. I like the flow and roll of the long passages, and I'm particularly fond of the final "Take 3," which appeared in 1987 on its own as "Eschatology Rant" in an underground journal called *Semiotext[e] USA*.

If you'd like to read a more comprehensive and factual version of my life, check out my autobiography, *Nested Scrolls*, published in 2011. And, yes, that book's title alludes to my composition method for *All the Visions*. My more mature memoir is, you might say, a full lifetime's accumulation of scrolls.

Anyway, back in 1983 I sliced my eighty-foot *All the Visions* scroll into page-sized pieces and mailed a copy to my friendly editor Gerard Van der Leun at the august house of Houghton Mifflin. As I mention in the text of *All the Visions*, Gerard mailed the manuscript right back. Our family dog Arf was a puppy then—he dragged the book off the porch and rolled in it. It was a week before I found the manuscript in the side yard, a "rainstained object of horror to the gods."

In 1991, my first edition of *All the Visions* was finally published as a slim volume in hardback and paperback from a small press, Lee Ballentine's Ocean View Books. It was bound back-to-back with *Space Baltic*, a collection of science-fictional poems by my far-out friend, Anselm Hollo, and with a cover by the great underground cartoonist Robert Williams.

In 1995, my musician friend Roy Whelden taped me reading some of the book and he backed the readings with baroque music, letting the celestial contralto Karen Clark sing some of the lyrics as well. The CD is called *Like A Passing River*, and the "Rucker Songs" cut includes telling passages from this book's "Take 3." Give us this day our daily rush, on the nod as thou art in heaven.

In 1983 I had no immediate hopes of seeing *All the Visions* published. Instead I used parts of the book as source material for my transreal SF novel, *The Secret of Life*. I should explain here that I use "transreal" to refer to novels that transmute the author's real life into science-fictional scenarios.

You might say that *Visions* and *Secret* are twin novels with the same characters…and the same goals. *The Secret of Life* is reappearing as part of my new collection, *Transreal Trilogy*.

Note also that *Transreal Trilogy* contains a list of my wonderful Kickstarter supporters—who funded these new editions. See www.rudydyrucker.com/allthevisions for further info.

And now—enjoy my visions!

—Rudy Rucker, June 20, 2014
Los Gatos, California

Take 1.

I was sixteen when it first hit me: someday you'll be dead. I was at a New Years Eve dance at the Riverview Country Club in Louisville, a much neater scene than I could ordinarily make—all the rich kids and hotshots there with pints of whiskey and cars and their own tuxedos. Me in my preacher-father's college tux and his horrible lumpy dress-shoes, but I didn't care once I found the cloak-room and patted down some overcoats and got my own pint-nip, the volatile fluid evaporating almost faster than I could gulp. What does it feel like to get drunk? I still ponder this, and try to put my finger on it, what does it feel like to be high?

Back at that 1962 Louisville party, I chugged my slugs and felt, oh, flushed skin and buzzing ears, and the sudden conviction that *I am cool*, regardless of what blank or hostile looks I might get. Climbing the stairs I could feel the passage of time, feel that the world was really going on. "I'm at the top of the stairs now," I thought, marveling and looking back down. "I'm right here now, and a second ago it seemed impossible for the steps ever to be over." I stepped into the Men's Room and stared at a urinal twelve feet away. "Now I'm here, and somehow I will, after, be over there." I crossed the room and pissed easefully, glad no big-dick was there to make me feel small. I stuck to my thought-train. "Last year I never thought I'd be drunk at a dance, yet here I am, just as surely as I've crossed this tile floor." Starting back for the door, the wider implications hit me. "I can't conceive of going to college, but that will come too, and when it comes it will just feel like now. I will go to college, and marry, and have children, and all the time it will be me doing it, me doing it in some mysteriously moving now. And then I'll die. It seems impossible, but some day I will really die."

I brooded over this for the next few weeks, and one Friday I got the car and went out cruising with my friend Jim Ardmore. We were in the same high-school fraternity, the Chevalier Literary Society. The Society had officers, and I was elected Critic, which meant that sometimes I would read a poem I admired, once the whole of "The Love Song of J. Alfred Prufrock," after which a fellow named Whale remarked that they had already covered that in his high-school English class. I read that poem some more in college, though now it's been awhile. Anyway, here's Ardmore and myself in my mother's VW Beetle, trying to get some booze.

There was one place way out on Route 42, a liquor store called Don's, and if you went out there either (a) Don himself might sell to you, or (b) some of the old black men in the back would go in for you, or (c) a soldier on leave from like Fort Knox would help you out. All three were dangerous or unlikely propositions, and I hit on the idea of getting wine from our church sacristy. I was a regular acolyte there, and knew (i) where the locked cabinet with the communion wine was, and (ii) where to find the key.

The church-building itself was unlocked, a really trusting and Christian way to have it. The fact that I may have stolen wine in no way denies the rightness of leaving the church unlocked *nevertheless*. The Church needs to be open for the sinner, and they can afford the wine for sure, cheap

California port in a cardboard case 12 bottles. Ardmore and me peering down at the wine, laughing high high-school laughs, "We're getting away with this!" I relocked the cabinet and put the key back in the drawer, and we took off back toward the city, chugging the shit and laughing. Pulled off on a special side-road to really slug it down, strong stuff, a whole quart, working on it, right away a cop-car pulls up. "Where did you boys get this wine?" cop says, sniffing it and like retching slightly at the smell, and then pouring it out on the road. "We got a soldier to buy it for us at Don's." Cop: "You're just lucky I caught you before you're drunk. Now go on where you're supposed to be and stay out of trouble."

So, dig it, we head right back to the church sacristy, get another quart, and drink this one driving up and down the Louisville highways…and the evening breaks into patches, stained glass windows, like, and one of them is me screaming at Ardmore, "We're going to die, Jim, can you believe it? It's really going to stop some day, all of it, and you're dead then, man, it's going to happen to you personally just like when I was at the dance and walking across the bathroom, how at the door I thought I'd never be at the sink, and then was there anyway. I can't stand it, I don't want to die, time keeps passing." Ardmore is laughing and laughing at this rap, never having seen me so animated, and for sure he's feeling the wine which we couldn't even finish all of. Then we were at a party of boys and girls our age in some guy's basement, low lights, cokes, records and I'm drunker than shit and talking about philosophy and deep questions and… for the first time people seem interested in hearing me. It's an act I've stayed with ever since. I have fun, you have fun, and the Church can afford it. Though of course my parents were mad, yelling at me, "Pig! Pig!"

Ah…pigs. When I was twelve my best school-days friend of all moved in behind us. Hank Larsen. Sundays there was never anything to do, and failing all else we'd walk along

Route 42 looking at things people had thrown out of their cars, hoping to find drugs or rubbers, walking a mile or two till we got to where a man raised mean pigs. We'd throw things at them and they'd squeal and charge us…anything to fill those huge empty Sundays.

Sometimes we'd have a wax-paper-wrapped pack of twenty firecrackers in our possession, and we'd ration them out, like life itself, the long yet finite progression to the urinal, modeled by the twenty-ness of the pack. Hank and I would set them off very judiciously, discussing and analyzing the placement of each successive charge of energy. The best effect ever was when I put a firecracker inside a cast-iron savings bank in the shape of a mail box, and the thing shattered into potentially maiming fragments, grenade-style, a teaching in itself.

From fireworks we moved on to rockets—this was in the late Fifties, shortly after the Russian sputnik. Hank and I had heard that good rocket-fuel is made of powdered zinc mixed with sulfur…but where do you score that on a Sunday in Louisville? Week after week we tested our substitute fuels. My insipid chemistry-set was useless, but match-heads worked pretty well. We'd fill up a plastic tube with them and watch them burn, just like a US rocket. It was the burning that counted, after all, not the flight. The best trick was to pour out pools of gasoline on our gravel driveway and light them. This was good, but even better was to take a shovelful of gravel, soak it in gasoline, light it, and then throw it high in the air. Sodom and Gomorrah, the wrath of God. Death was still just a movie. But not for my parents. They caught us with the gasoline, and hearing that we really wanted to build rockets, they bought me a fine fine toy called Alpha-One.

The Alpha-One was a red plastic rocket with two chambers, a solid-fuel chamber and a liquid-fuel chamber. The solid fuel was some kind of white crystal, and the liquid fuel made the crystals foam up. The two would stay separate until you sealed the rocket. Then they would mix and release a jet of gas that threw the rocket a hundred feet, as high as the Chinese elm tree in our front yard. Soon the fuel was gone and the Alpha-One rocket company was out of business. Hank wanted to fill the rocket with match-heads. I suggested baking-powder. Mixing it with vinegar wasn't quite strong enough, but then we hit on hydrogen peroxide for the liquid-fuel. This worked very well, so well that we got bored. I used the rest of the peroxide to bleach my hair. The girls liked it, but the barber didn't. "Hey, look, we've got a two-tone," he called, when I went for a trim. Blond on top and brown on the sides. Long hair came later, and the cranky barbers would say, "Hey, look, we've got a Beatle."

What a salvation the hippie thing was for all of us! The agony of week after week in high-school reading about the beatniks in *Time* magazine and knowing you were missing out on being really neat, reading about existentialists and the Angry Young Men…in high school Hank and I would devour the occasional anthologies of these writers we'd find in the Louisville Free Public Library. We're all going to die, right! And these guys are doing something about it, doing something to fill up the endless Louisville Sunday with noise and visions and drunkenness and drugs.

In my big brother's bookcase we came across an old *Evergreen Review* story about eating Benzedrine inhalers, and borrowed my mother's VW to go to a big downtown drugstore and get some, and even though the inhalers were already FDA safe, Benzedrex, man, and really like only camphor, we spent one Saturday party cracking 'em, eating the strips, and pretending to be high. Which is a high of sorts of course, I was still reeling when I got home, and my parents were waiting up for me, ready to yell, "Pig! Pig!" but slyly saying "Come kiss us goodnight, Conrad," and as I kiss the slick withered cheeks they *sssniffff* for the beer-smell but this one psych-high fake-benny time they could only shake their heads in wonder, "He's as clean as the new-driven snow." "Why do you wait up for me?" I'd yell in anguish. "Some day you'll have children of your own and you'll understand."

Children of my own? Yes, of course, I knew from metaphysical grounds that this was surely true, but to have children you have to find some woman who will fuck you which seemed...well...the possibility of me getting laid seemed so unlikely that I almost longed for nuclear war. Why? Because then there would be a lot of *dead women* lying around and maybe I could find a fresh one and undress her and see everything and even do it. Not that I wanted especially to fuck a corpse, mind you, it was just that it seemed like the best shot I was ever going to get.

All through my early high-school years I was somehow teamed up with a blonde girl named Linda, a tennis player who I went steady with. I dated only her and she dated only me. Did we like each other? Well, hey, she was like the only girl I'd ever managed to talk to—I went to an all-boys school, you know. I'd met this girl in dancing school. We sleepwalked along together, holding hands and kissing... sometimes I'd lie on part of her...but later, when I was a senior and I tried to tell Linda about death, it was over, and we were relieved. She could date other tennis-stars and I...I could try to go out with a girl who was hot.

Hot girls. One had a body that made a loud noise when I'd lie on her—fully clothed, you understand, and the mosquitoes buzzing around the parked car, and her body somehow making a noise like a drain. *Graaah-gurrh.* I assumed all girls were like that and neglected to research the symptom's etiology. "We mustn't make out like this Conrad." "OK."

Hot girls. Another let me slide my hand under her girdle—a sixteen-year-old girl with a big ass and a girdle so tight that when you'd pat one cheek, the other cheek would like echo the pat and wag-wag too. But sliding the hand under the girdle was hopeless, the confusing hair and slick surfaces, and the feeling steadily draining from my fingers under the pressure of the tight elastic. And as it turned out, she only liked to date me if we could double with my pal Hank, tall blonde Hank Larsen.

Hank and I were a Mutt and Jeff team, him about six feet, me about five feet and...face it, me a weenie more or less, longing to be cool. But we had science fiction in common, and the vague longing for beer and drugs and sex, a passion for the cheap thrills of the annual state fair, and the endless idle days of summer, exploring the new tract-homes going up all around us as Louisville suburbia grew eastward. The workmen would be gone on most Saturdays and Sundays, and then we could piss on the blueprints, climb on top of the framed-up walls, look for nickel-shaped slugs from the electrical boxes, and feed leftover lunches to my dog Muffin.

My parents had built one of the first suburban houses in our area, its walls and ceilings made of that modern wonder-material: plywood. They'd moved in after renting a series of places, the earliest being a big creaky house on an old farm. At some point that farm closed down and the owners auctioned everything off. One of my first memories is of that auction day, I guess I was two.

> I'm high up on a piece of machinery. It's yellow.
> I can see the tops of the grownups' heads. One
> of them smiles up at me, calling me by name.
> "Conrad." Somehow his arms reach the huge
> distance up to where I perch on the tractor's
> metal seat, and he lifts me down.

As a teen, suddenly aware of death, I'd sift through the few bright childhood memories, wondering why I would remember this or that, shuffling through these few bright fragments of childhood infinity. What do they mean, these few leftover visions?

> Behind our house is a rye-field. The rye is taller than me. I walk through it, tramping down labyrinths. In the fall the rye is cut. The farmer's tractor has been sold, his house is deserted. Another boy and I walk across the field and begin breaking windows with rocks. I hit one window and the shattered black hole is the exact shape of the Pontiac Indian, hard-nosed profile and long feathers in back. A black man runs out and yells at us. We run and run and run.

Nursery school is held in a big room at the church. Giant wood blocks are piled up higher than my head. One of the children takes me aside and points out one of the others. "Look out for him. He's called Butch." Later I'm on the toilet and two little girls come in. "Get out of here," I tell them, "Can't you read? This bathroom says MEN." "No it doesn't," they insist. We argue and argue. At least I have my stall door locked. Printed on the porcelain of the toilet is the word CHURCH.

I'm home in time for lunch every day. Mom often treats me to a special lunch of spaghetti and lambchop. After lunch I sit on her lap and she hugs and kisses me. Muffin watches, looking dog-mournful. "Look at Muffy," I say. "Muffy feels left out." Then I take my nap.

I never got soft drinks except at birthday parties, and only one lollipop a week, purchased by my mother at the A&P. I barely knew what candy was, but each morning I had to take a powerful depressant drug: Benadryl, a type of antihistamine. My mother worried I might have an asthma attack, so I spent much of my childhood numb on a downer. Well, it was the Fifties, everyone was on downers, it seemed like.

Some wealthy friends of my parents had a grown son, a man named Lennox, he was an artist, one of the few in Louisville, a painter whom my mother engaged to give me art lessons. He was a fascinatingly messy man, with a pocket-handkerchief daubed with every color on his palette. I got to see a show of his pictures once, all seascapes, competently done.

Two girls took art lessons from Lennox with me, one wore a back-brace—she'd had polio, I liked her, she was smart. She hinted around that she wanted to see my penis, but I pretended not to understand. The other girl had a blonde pony-tail and laughed a lot. Her name was Julie and she lived in a house with a flat roof. The girl with the back-brace said that I had a crush on Julie. That sounded right to me. I dreamed of being crushed together with Julie. Lennox gave art lessons to other groups of children as well, not that he needed the money, being a millionaire's son, but he needed something to do. Or maybe he liked meeting the children's mothers. A confirmed bachelor. His clothes were so filthy and paint-spotted that I often wondered what his room must be like. One day Lennox showed up with peanut butter on one shoulder. "One of my other students did that," he complained. "Just because I was friendly, she took her peanut-butter-and-jelly sandwich in half and stuck it to my face. I don't think that's right."

I sometimes think Lennox was in love with my mother, she herself being something of an artist. But I'm sure she never responded to his hypothetical advances, if only because his clothes were so dirty. He talked Mom into paying him to paint my portrait. I sat for hours and hours, and he kept changing the picture and messing it up and having to start over. "I can't do noses," he would affably tell me, rubbing wet paint off the canvas with his sleeve. After a few weeks he gave up on doing an oil and went to pastels. Finally the picture was finished, even the nose, and he gave me a cheap baseball glove for sitting so long. He and Mom sent me outside to play. Maybe that was Lennox's chance to put a move on Mom. Occasionally Lennox would give me a ride to the group art lessons, and when we were alone together, he'd tell me dirty jokes. He called women's breasts "headlights." Looking back, I'd say that Lennox looked and talked like my future hero Jack Kerouac. He told me that he'd once seen a woman pissing under a bridge, and he cackled with joy as he recalled this. He was a volunteer fireman and he had a real siren on his car, but he was unwilling to turn it on except for a real fire—he was worried that if he misused the siren they would take it away from him. My mother still has the pastel Lennox did of me. A nice little boy with brown eyes. The nose is wrong, though.

Eventually it was time to enroll me in dancing school. An old lady ran it, and my ninth-grade algebra teacher played the role of bouncer. At the beginning of each class we were supposed to pair up. The girls would be along one wall, in dresses and with white gloves, and the boys along the other wall. "Choose your partners!" the old lady would call, and you'd have to go over and ask a girl to dance. If you didn't pick one, my burr-cut algebra teacher would pick for you—so it was just as well to go ahead and get it over with.

The sharp boys asked the sharp girls and the rest of us did the best we could. Once I danced with a girl who said her name was "Tray," and she kept saying bad words. "Take your position," said the old teacher, for instance, and this partner Tray would giggle and say, "*Piss*-ition, get it?" I could hardly believe my ears. I only got to dance with her once. After awhile I began dancing regularly with Linda. She was blonde and pleasant and played tennis and, as I mentioned, I ended up going steady with her through most of high school. In dancing school Linda often wore a bracelet with all kinds of nuts on it, which gave us some-thing to talk about. "I see you have your bracelet with the nuts on again." "That's right." "I wonder what kind of nut that light brown one is?" "I don't know. Maybe it's from South America?" Later, when I'd take Linda to the movies, my father would drive us. Linda and I would sit in back together, and whenever my father said anything, she would sort of scream and say, "Yessir." Linda's mother had once sat on my father's lap at a party. The two geezers both liked reminiscing about it.

Linda's big sister Bunny had been very into riding, as so many Louisville girls were. I have a horror of horses, fostered by the fact that a horse at our neighbor Mr. Skelton's farm kicked me in the leg right near my balls when I was ten, very scary. Linda's big sis Bunny had run off with a stable-groom, eloped and married him, and the family was so freaked about it they raised Linda as an only child, never mentioning the big sister at all. Linda's family lived in a lovely old house that had once been the home of President Zachary Taylor. It had a secret passage that, Linda claimed, led all the way to the nearby graveyard where Zachary Taylor and his wife are buried, along with about five thousand dead WWII soldiers.

One night Linda's parents weren't home, and I came over. We kissed a lot and then decided to do something bad. I got a can of paint and a brush from her basement, and we walked around daubing crude graffiti on the suburban streets. I wanted to make people mad. So that no one would suspect Linda, I defaced her parents' asphalt driveway as well. Excited by our little rebellion, I asked Linda if she would have sex with me—OK, maybe not right now, but would she do it with me in the afterworld after death? She didn't care to commit herself even to that.

Linda made me take her to every Doris Day movie that ever came to Louisville. Often she would already have seen the movie at a matinee, but would pretend not to have seen it, so that she could go again, but once we were in the movie she'd tell me. She knew how to wrinkle her nose just like Doris Day. I imprinted on Doris Day like a baby duck following the first thing it sees move. They say Doris Day is kind of eccentric now, and lives with a whole lot of dogs. I don't care, I still love her. In four years I don't think I ever touched Linda's breasts. The very last time she went out with me, I got drunk and threw up. "Linda, we're all going to die and everything is meaningless." "Huh?"

Somehow high school itself was over one day, and I was asleep in the back of my parents' car. They were driving me up to Philadelphia to go to Swarthmore College. My roommate, I saw from the list, was from Brooklyn. Ron Platek. Outside our dorm, I saw a confused black kid, and I assumed that was Platek. I was sure anyone from Brooklyn would be black. But Ron was tall, crew-cut, stooped, Jewish. Ron, for his part, had expected that anyone named "Conrad von Riemann Bunger" would be busy tacking up swastikas as soon as he showed up.

I had never even met any Jewish people in Louisville, or even thought about them at all, so I was surprised when one day Ron wouldn't eat anything. "It's Yom Kippur." Me: "What's that?" Gradually I realized that nearly all of my new friends and classmates were Jewish—I'd just thought of them as dark guys with curly hair. To some extent they were intrigued by me being half-German, which made me exotic and suspect from their point of view. Izzy Tuskman would chant, "Einstein, Marx, and Freud," goading me, hoping for some titillating display of prejudice. And Izzy's roommate Chuckie Golem would loll back against the wall, legs crossed, arms outspread, and say, "Some of us are pretty nice guys," meaning Jesus himself. Not that religion was much of an issue for me. It was all bullshit anyway.

Ron Platek and I became good friends, and we'd have

great long evenings together, each of us in bed, talking across the dark room about the visions we'd had, the things we'd dreamed. I told him about death, and he got properly agitated, "I can't believe all this will stop," he cried. "Me going places and seeing new things, how can it ever end?" Platek's exaggerated woe made the whole thing seem funny, like a practical joke he really deserved, and never mind that the same prank was in store for me. I liked pranks.

One night freshman year I managed to get the drunkest I'd ever been, starting with a bottle from a sophomore student who made his only friends by scoring for freshmen, and ending with some mature fraternity guy walking me around outside to finish throwing up. My roommate Ron wasn't quite yelling, "Pig! Pig!" but he was pretty grossed out. The next day I'm too beat to get dressed properly and I just pull a pair of pants over the pajamas my mother sent me off with. Go to the dining-hall for breakfast, and right after, I'm puking off the porch. Some prospective students with parents walk by, frowning over at me, and I think, hey, I'm a grown-up degenerate now, a real college boy, just like those mysterious people I'd seen sitting in jeans on the lawn during the big college-tour the year before.

There were classes too, of course, but they all seemed so off the mark. Philosophy was a particular disappointment, and finally I ask the professor, "Aren't we going to talk about death and big questions instead of the-knower-and-the-known?" He laughs kindly, "I felt the same way myself." The worst of all was the required Political Science course. "I think we're all liberal democrats here, aren't we?" says the professor, and me and the other Southern boy raise our hands to say, *No.* The other boy is a conservative. And me: "I'm an anarchist." "Anarchy is not a political stance," raps out the professor, and I'm happily alienated a notch further.

The best thing at college is the girls. All through high-school I've been, for some reason, at an all-male Catholic school. St. X. My parents thought it had the best science program. The other boys at St. X. had been unable to clearly perceive the difference between a Protestant and a Jew: "The Jew," they'd call me. "Why did you kill Jesus?" The worst was when they'd decide to baptize me, meaning corner me in the bathroom and yell at me and throw water on me. Boys having fun. But at college there were girls everywhere and, it being Swarthmore, the girls were not necessarily the hard-shelled beauties of the South, no, these were real people you could talk to. And talk. The first girl I dated had grown up in the West Village in New York, a solid woman. She said, "Please don't call me an earth mother." I charmed her by telling her that my brother Caldwell had committed suicide on Christmas morning by pulling the trigger of a shot-gun with his big toe.

In fact, my brother was in the army at this point, and very much alive. He'd been booted out of his college for—I never quite got the clear story—but something like breaking open a beer warehouse at dawn and sniping at the cops with a .22 rifle. When Caldwell was sent back to Louisville, my father took him to "meet someone," who turned out to be the army recruiter. He was older and cooler than me, my brother—he even had a subscription to the *Evergreen Review*, and had all those back issues that I used to look through for, first, sex material, and, later, for art, for answers to the void at the center of US existence, and also for drug tips, as I already mentioned. So I knew enough to act reasonably cool, and could charm even a girl from New York City, play it cool or play it country, whatever worked best. And talk and talk. But somehow, impossibly, I was never any closer to real nookie than in high school.

Really it was always brain-ecstasy that was my quest, rather than sex-scores. Like in Louisville once, at a rock-and-roll show with my Chevalier Literary Society buddies, one of them says, "I'm going to get some stuff," and I holler,

"Hey, get me a half-pint!" and the guy looks at me pityingly, "Conrad, girls don't come in half-pints." Those rock and roll shows were so great, they'd get all the bands with hits, all on tour together. Memory-flash of me walking slowly, thoughtfully through an empty section of bleachers while listening to Del Shannon sing the poignant "Raindrops," his falling tears like raindrops, yes. And Bo Diddley himself there with his band, jiving with a sideman. "Hey! I hear yo Daddy a light-bulb eater." "He ain't be no ligh'-bu'b eater." "Sho. Every time he turn off the bedroom light he *eat* a little piece." During the intermission I hurried down to see Bo in person. He was behind the stage, shorter than I'd imagined. "Are you Bo Diddley?" "Yes." "Can I shake your hand?" Bo *Diddley*. He was the start of music for me. Hank and I, between us, had all his albums, and if my parents were ever out of town we'd get our dates and listen over and over, exclaiming at the musical elegance and the richness of Bo's wit.

Nobody at Swarthmore had heard of Bo Diddley, it seemed like, they were all into Bob Dylan, and lots of them had guitars and would play folk-songs on the porch after dinner. These were considered the neat people, the porch-sitters. My first college girlfriend, the non-earth-mother, left me for a porch-sitter. My next girl was also from New York, and wanted to hear about debutante balls. I had not been to any, but big brother Caldwell had, so I used his second-hand memories to fake it as best I could. At least I'd been to the senior-prom breakfast, with the girl whose body sometimes made that alarming noise and I'd managed to throw up after only two too-fast beers. College would be more fun than high school, I was sure. And towards the end of my college freshman year I met the girl I ended up marrying, Audrey Hayes.

My parents had moved from Louisville to Washington, D.C. just before I went away to college. Talk about uprooting!

25

The last morning before we left Louisville, I got up about six and went over to Hank' Larsen's house. We each had a frozen cream pie that we'd left out on our kitchen counters all night. The idea was that for the good-bye we'd each shove a pie into the other's face. But we just stood there with our sad, flat frozen pies, stood there staggered at the arrival of the end of childhood. Talk about a death-hit! Whew! Anyway, at spring vacation during my freshman year of college, I rode down to D.C. on a bus the college had chartered. There was a nice-looking girl in one of the seats: bouffant hair-do, lipstick, Peter Pan collar. "Can I sit here?" I say. "Do you mind if I smoke?" she asks. She smoked Newports. I'd just learned to smoke recently, standing out after the meals with the porch-sitters strumming away, drag on the cig and get a…dizzy feeling, a definite up. I had my *New York Times* with me on the bus, I'd learned to smoke and to read the *Times* up north, and I found something in it to talk to my seat-mate about. It was an article about how many people get killed by shocks from electric eels every year in the mouth of the Amazon River. Three per year on the average, but this year was running high. Two more of us were being jolted right now, sitting there in the bus, talking talking, like about Pop Art and about the long, long, imaginary scythe that, when you're riding, reaches invisibly out into the landscape and has to jump over phone poles and over cars, but maybe you cut down a pedestrian or two…it doesn't have to be a scythe, it can be a little running man who hops, or even a machine-gun. "Not a machine-gun," says Audrey, slightly thrilled.

She'd even read Sartre's *Nausea*, which had been a biggie for Hank and me the year before. For months I'd tried wearing that book's personality—like an ill-fitting beret in some kid's Halloween "beatnik" costume. Sartre's feeling of disgust at the tenacious *is-ness* of things, the persistence of the *real*, ugh. What really bugged me more, though, as I've mentioned, and as I told Audrey, was the passage of time, the fact that step after step was happening and before long— bang, you're dead. "God is dead, all is permitted," I'd chanted into open microphones at those high-school dances—ah, just another badly made beret or WWII German helmet.

I was so ecstatic about meeting Audrey that I forgot to get her name. Back at Swarthmore after spring vacation, it took me a week or two to find her again…she was two years ahead of me, a junior, so we didn't run in the same circles. Finally I saw her over the condiment table, where they set out bowls of ketchup, mustard, mayo, relish, oil, vinegar, peanut butter. It actually took ten dates till we kissed. Maybe subconsciously I knew there was no rush, with all the years together ahead. Consciously, of course, I was impatient, disgusted with myself for not being more aggressive. At the first kiss, I'd bought her a cone of strawberry ice cream and we were in some inane, tense argument about who would lick it first, neither of us really thinking about the ice cream at all, and I just dropped it on the ground and *kiss*. We walked away from the lights and kiss kissed again again. We kissed a lot, for as long as an hour sometimes, standing in the hall of her dorm, the endless slow tongue friction, the sweet smell of her, my sobbing hard-on in my tight undies…ah those years of slow happy courtship, and the college beer parties in the woods together, and then parties without her as she graduated and went off to grad school.

Money was always a problem, money for beer, and later for trips to visit Audrey. I'd borrow from a kind old college secretary—the loan being an advance against the monthly allowance my parents would send me. And I'd found a way to make my dorm's payphone disgorge extra change. I just had to thump it in a certain way. And there was an isolated and decrepit soft-drink machine with a broken latch that let you score a couple of dollars of change from the coin box once in awhile, if someone else hadn't gotten there first. The machine was in the basement of my new friend Ace Weston's dorm. I met Ace sophomore year. I was living in a quad then, four boys together: me, a black, a Jew, and a preppie…one of each, a regular *Sgt. Rock Comics* platoon. Ace used to come to my quad to drink with me. We'd get a case of beer every Saturday. What bliss, a whole case of beer for the two of us, talking about how charming and witty we were, and saying that if everyone could just see us right now, see us the way we saw each other, why then they'd love us as much as we loved ourselves. "Cast Your Fate To The Wind" by the Vince Guaraldi Trio on eternal repeat on my plastic record-player, and in the distance people yelling at a football game.

Football? Get serious! There were visions to be had here, beer visions, and adventure…like the throwing-knife I had, a flat-stamped piece of metal, really, and Ace and I would endlessly practice throwing it at the back of my room's door, missing sometimes and chunking the wall. The worst of throws was the "death-clanger" when the knife would hit hard on the handle-end and twist whirring back through the startled air to jab at the thrower. My roommates didn't like this, there was tension, once to "get even" I locked the room and climbed out the window with Ace, leaving my 45 record of "Surfin Bird" on eternal repeat. There was a classics major across the hall—he used to write plays about Antigone and the House of Atreus in blank verse, horrible plays, and he hated "Surfin Bird," clawing at my door and moaning *Stop*, but I had to be bad, wanted to be a hood, really, after all my high-school fears of tough guys. Swarthmore was such an academic school that everyone there was as much of or even more of a weenie as me. Ace was into the trip, too, us being bad boys, scary madmen, dumb assholes really, frightened children. It was amazing to think that here at college I could be a hot shot, without

joining a fraternity of course—it was the Sixties now, just
beginning, though we didn't quite realize it, and fraternities
were nowhere. But of course we had our cliques, boys and
girls together, it was the coed high school I'd missed out
on by going to St. X Boys High.

The drugs finally showed up junior year, although there
had been a kind of brush with them my first year. A pretty
girl I'd talked to had told me that she knew some boys who
took peyote. So to, I don't know, make her uptight or to
make something happen, I crushed an aspirin and put the
white powder in a tight little case and typed, "H. For more,
phone…" For the number I put the pay-phone in my dorm.
So two days later, the girl phoned up, excited and frightened,
and by then I'd kind of forgotten and didn't say anything,
and then the next day a guy, a non-student, shows up at my
room, having done a detective trip, looking through the
college phone directory to figure out my dorm, and then
matching the note's typing to the typing on the nametag I'd
put on our room's door. "I'm Nick. Did you send heroin?"
Me: "No, that was just aspirin, I was just kidding." Nick: "I
snorted it I and thought I got a rush." "No, no."

He drifted out again, though two years later I learned
his friend Freddy Whitman had flipped so bad over the
scare that he'd spent two days lying in bed staring at an
imaginary neon H-E-R-O-I-N light. Freddy told me this
when I met him junior year, I'd heard he was a big druggie,
and one day I sauntered half-drunk into his room, "I am
the prophet of alcohol come to meet the prophet of drugs."
Freddy had these round steel-rimmed glasses, and always
an unbuttoned button-down collar shirt with the sleeves
rolled high up over his elbows, the elbows jerking out to
the sides *make room, make room*, chuckling and working
on incomprehensible letters to, like, the FBI to leave him
alone. Or studying, frame by frame, a Marvel Comic. "This
one is about a trip, man, you see how the guy gets on the

abandoned subway and it's full of monsters?"

That was indeed the trip I got one morning when I fall by Freddy's room, and he gets out a cardboard box of peyote buds. "These come from Texas, the Wild Zag Ranch, you send off for them, they're still legal. Spit out the hairs when you chew, the hairs have strychnine." I'm chewing the stuff, feeling myself passing through an interface, this is real. Freddy was making me nervous, jerking his elbows and peering at me, so I went down to the lobby to phone Audrey, off at grad school in New York City by now. But I took some wrong turn and I'm on Freddy's subway with the monsters, right in the front, watching the ropey tooth-monsters coming at me in waves, brown and yellow all down the sides of a black-green tunnel. Waves of, like, contractions are sweeping over me, waves and monsters. At some point I realize that what I'm doing is throwing up into a waste basket and staring at the vomit patterns. I've been throwing up for a half hour maybe. "You have to get help," I think, and the thought repeats in my head in tiny sped-up voices, *help help help*, then shatters into wicked laughter, it's just like the nightmare I had over and over when I was tiny: *A circus lit by darkly smoldering torches. High overhead fly the acrobats, creatures of light, devils. I run upstairs and hide behind a pile of doors.*

There's no pile of doors now, though, just the empty midday street, college-town empty, and the leafless leaning trees are clawed hands above the sidewalk. "Relax, Conrad, it's just the drug," I tell myself. *Relax*, pipe the head-voices, *relaxlaxlalahah ahahahahaaaaaaa*! I find my way to my room, but nobody's there, and everything...looks like a face, the sink *chuckle chuckle*, the wall *snf snf*, the door *helloooo*. I run out and find finally a house with friends, three or four of them, me trying to explain, but they soon get the picture, and in my head everything is all cut up and collaged, memories from the past and from the future—suddenly I'm already a college professor lecturing on relativity theory! Sitting at the table talking or making noises as my friends solemnly watch, how I love them. Then into the living room—this shit is like being shot out of a cannon, if I close my eyes I'm a pinball in a high-score game, and if I open them, "I'm in a Renoir!" My voice sounds sweet and sticky, but I have to tell it. "I've always loved Renoir, and now everything looks like one of his paintings!" "Where did you get this stuff, Conrad?"

They find Ron Platek, who's still rooming with me, and I go back to sit on a chair in our room with him, watching as his face segues through *click-click-click* a slideshow of the whole history of Western art: primitive, cubist, impressionist, comic, *click*. Outside some trees still have their leaves, red and yellow. I close my eyes, I'm in my head with flecks of blue red yellow, a big balloon of color floating up higher and higher from the earth, a thinner and thinner tube connecting me back to earth and… "It's going to break!" I cry in panic. "The thread is going to break and I'll be dead." Ron: "No, no, just relax." Me: "Promise me that if I stop breathing you'll wake me up." Ron tires of this and sets me loose. I go to Ace's room and try to tell him about it. "You been freaking out?" he muses, looking at me, then hunches over like an evil caveman to snarl and threaten. "Don't," I scream, "My brain will pop!" He relents and we go to supper.

The next day I go to New York to sleep with Audrey at her grad school apartment. She shares it with two other girls, Katha and Elizabeth. Elizabeth is weird, a budding social worker who's never ever dreamed of being cool. Her idea of a fun thing is that we all get on the subway and… run up to the front car and stare out (oh no) at the black tunnel ahead with the ropey tooth-monsters that only I can see. I told Audrey about it and she was sad. "Your drinking is already so bad—why start on drugs? It's seedy."

Coming back to my dorm after New York, I keep looking at my hands to see the flesh fall off, I see the bones, the skeleton. Wow.

There's no trip like that first one. Freddy was the only serious doper on campus, and he offered me some red liquid mescaline that he'd cooked out of the peyote, but now I was scared. Some weed showed up and we all learned how to do that—although actually fearing, in our youth, the madness in a reefer, "I hope I don't freak out."

Freaking out. All the ways of freaking out, all the ways of being high. There was a period when I couldn't tell the difference between freaking out and being high—or pretended that I couldn't—this was in graduate school, me finally having to buckle down and get good grades and, surprisingly, being able to get them. I never got an A in college, but in grad school you had to, my dear, for now it was your ass. So much of my confusion cleared up at once. The peak of it was 1972, that was the big Sixties year for me, and it was about as smart as I ever got. Like finally waking up out of the chrysalis and being able to… *do*, as P. D. Ouspensky puts it. I discovered Ouspensky in a library—typical exciting event in a scholar's life, "I found a neat book." It was *Tertium Organum*, involving discussions of the fourth dimension and…wait, am I done with childhood and college yet? Let's go back in the memory church and look at three more of those stained-glass windows.

Sometimes I'm sick, and I stay in bed all day. The doctor comes with a black bag and maybe a shot of penicillin. When Pop gets home from work looks in on me. "How's my sausage? Look out for the bumble-bee!" He buzzes and moves his hand in circles—then puts a quarter on the tip of his left forefinger, then snaps the fingers of his right hand. The quarter disappears up his right sleeve. He pretends to find it in my ear and lets me keep it.

In the summer I learn to swat flies. One afternoon I go

out on our concrete back steps and swat flies for a whole hour. More and more of them come, attracted by the bodies of their squashed comrades. I call my mother to admire what I've done. "Don't you ever do that again."

The kindergarten teacher drives by our house on her way to school, so I get a ride with her every day. I stand alone, out by the highway, and she stops for me. She wears a lot of lipstick, which gets all over the cigarettes she smokes. Her car is a Buick Dynaflow with fake portholes in the side. I know they're fake by checking with my finger.

I finally got a car like that, a '56 Buick Century. Black on the bottom and with a white roof, I gave it to Audrey for her big birthday a few months ago, in February, 1983. Snuck it into our driveway and in the morning I handed her the grotty old key, man! We all ran out in our pajamas. Audrey: "I want to start it! I want to drive it!" And we motored around the block, her and me and the three grubbers.

We have three kids, yeah, let's get into that later, they're beautiful, but right now I want to wallow in the deeper past, talking about my brother Caldwell. He was five years older than me, a buck-toothed gangler, a friend and a hero. He had a black suit that he wore with a pink shirt and a black knit tie and he got beat up at the Plantation Swimming Club for cutting off a guy while he (Caldwell) was driving a big old Indian brand motorcycle that he'd borrowed off the cool assistant minister at our church.

Last time I saw Caldwell, just a couple of months ago, he has a new motorcycle, an antique Harley, and he wants to take me out on a drive. "Sure." I can see the little round speedometer over his shoulder, it has the numbers one through twelve. It's on seven, and I say, "That's fast enough." "I like round numbers, Conrad." "Seventy's a round number." Chuckle, chuckle and it's up to 10, everything vibrating, the landscape gone into aether, feeling like Wilbur and Frank Lloyd Wright. My big brother. The great lies he told me when we were younger—you know how kids like to trick their ignorant grubber younger siblings.

(1) Caldwell has several teeth saved in his drawer. He says that he found them in front of our house. He says that a dentist used to lived here and that the dentist threw people's teeth out the window after pulling them. I search for teeth in the yard, but find only a clover-like plant which tastes nice and sour.

(2) There's a peach tree in our front yard. Caldwell and I stand under the tree, wondering if it will ever bear fruit. He says that one year it did. Just then a very strange plane flies overhead, a plane with no fuselage, a sort of huge metal boomerang. "That's a Flying Wing," Caldwell tells me. The next day we go outside, hoping to see the Flying Wing again. Instead we find two strange kids in our yard, kids with Comanche haircuts. Mohawks. Caldwell hits the big one, and they go away.

(3) We're driving south through the mountains. A sharp bend with "GET RIGHT WITH GOD!" on a sign at a scree-scree corner. We're sick to our stomachs, we're yelling for fireworks, fireworks, and Caldwell tells me that tomorrow we will be on the Skyline drive which has, like, suspended bridge spans from mountain top to mountain top, a level road over the mountain peaks. "Is that true, Mom, is that true?" "Oh, sure, now take a nap why don't you?"

(4) The next day the road's still winding and winding, and Caldwell has to take a shit. He disappears into the woods, and after awhile he comes whooping back to the car. "You ought to see my turd. It's this long, and green with red pimples on it!" "Let's go see, Pop, let's go see!" "Get in the car!"

Those family trips…the wee-wee bottle my brother and I would have to piss in, an empty Coke usually, so that the parents didn't have to stop so often. When the wee-wee bottle got full, you poured it out the window and it made big streams…like flames, really, all along our beige station-wagon. *Flaaaames*, baby, *flaames*.

After grad school when I got my first teaching job, my dad bought me and Audrey a white Ford, and I flamed the mother. Before I somehow came into my own in 1972, I couldn't have done such a thing myself, although I would gladly have helped my brother do it. With my Ford, I put blue flames on one side, and red on the other, with yellow centers and black outlines, all freehand, very large, coming out of the front wheel-wells and flickering along the full length of the car, rude and crude. Everybody said the flames would ruin the car's resale value, but when the time came it sold all right…the guy just repainted it. The flames came from Caldwell's influence for sure. He was the last of the Fifties, and I was the first of the Sixties. Caldwell's library was poised at the interface: stacks of hot-rod magazines and, like I keep mentioning, his shelves of *Evergreen Review*.

Here's an entry from my young-writer diary from twenty years ago, my parents were leaving Louisville to move to the D.C. area and then I was going off to college. I had a girlfriend named Taffy that summer. So here we go, an archival diary entry that I might entitle with the *I Ching* phrase, "Difficulties at the Beginning."

> *September 2, 1963.* It is a hot humid oppressive day and I have to play golf with Pop. I get along pretty well with my parents, I just don't talk to them much usually—when I stopped going to church we had a huge screaming cursing weeping argument. I can't talk to my father too well since he always is disapproving or judging me. Every action is obviously meaningless, I do not see how I ever felt otherwise—we die dead and completely, what difference does anything make against that fact?…I wish I could get rid

of my fucking bastard pimples…

Well, hey, I was only seventeen, and it's true, isn't it? The point about death negating all of life, no, that's not true, is it? Here's a week later, my last day in Louisville.

> *September 11, 1963.* Everything is over—the years with Hank, the years of school, the weeks with Taffy, all my familiarity and comfort with my surroundings. It is so hard to change and now after four years of hard work in college [*Ha!*] I will have to make my own living…

Enough, enough, these "gems" were written into a pocket-size diary book that someone gave me in 1960, a little jobbie that, even now, I've only filled as far as some pages that are printed with dates from June, 1960. There's a year's worth of space in the little book and I have a horror of finishing it, of exhausting it—for then (it could be argued) I will croak. June's no sweat though, that's like mid-summer, the sixth month.

Up here in real time—I'm typing this on my Jack Kerouac scroll of paper, bought yesterday at the stationers, it's like a giant roller towel, equals 675 sheets end-to-end of normal typing paper, not that I'll use the full scroll—up here it's June 22, 1983, the day after the longest day of the year. Given that the standard appointed life-span is 72 years, which equals 12 times 6, that means that the "year" of a human lifespan is 12 "months" of 6 years each, so that the metaphorical sixth month of "June" reaches life-year 36, and I'm 37, which is *near* the end of "June," you understand—so in my life and in that old pocket-diary and in the real world, in *all three*, today is late June, June, June, line up the sights and pull the trigger: I'm writing *All the Visions* at last. This is a very exposed place to be, the real-time present. The only place, too, oh who cares. Be here now.

What about death? Have I found an answer to death after all these years? Yes, I have answers, but maybe they're incomprehensible. Death is simple, but my evasions are complex. One approach is to deny the passage of time, so that the fact that one lives 72 years is no sadder than the fact that one is 72 inches tall. (71-and-a-half inches, really, in my case.) Or, second approach, one can argue that, on the fundamental reality level, all physical existence is lit farts on a subway. Ropey tooth-monster God out there? Naw, it's pulsing energy nodes. Is the Aphrodite present in an uncarved block of marble? I thought so, maybe, during that old peyote trip, humping, I think, an ice-box, and lecturing on Special Relativity. I'm eternally a potential pattern, and therefore immortal.

Life is so long, life is so short. The enemies: divorce, madness, suicide, disease. "If you're going to die anyway, then nothing matters." Is that right? "Since this meal is going to be over anyway it might as well be roast shit instead of Wienerschnitzel." "Since this song is going to be over anyway it might as well be Mantovani dentist supermarket airport strings went the zing of my heart." "Since this turd will be flushed it might as well be green with red pimples." "Since this is America, a movie-actor might as well be president." Process, process. We are here for a time to grow and bloom—hey *do* it. I mean...have some fun.

That last sentence is from a guy who'd been in the Navy in Viet-Nam, riding up and down the rivers on a gunboat, and seeing his friends get popped off. I met him down in the Turks and Caicos Islands in the Caribbean. Audrey and the kids and I were visiting brother Caldwell, who was living there. After the Army, Caldwell had gotten Pop to buy him endless plane-lessons, and now he had a commercial pilot's license, and he was flying planes for Turks and Caicos Airways. So my little family and I went down there, escaping the lousy, cold, wet spring of upstate New York, where I was teaching math at Bernco State College—oh god, the years of grubbing for tenure there! *Yaaaah!*

This trip to Grand Turk was right after my thirtieth birthday party, where all my old friends came, and I even paid some of their plane tickets with the thousand dollars I got for my little non-fiction 4D book I'd managed to publish, *Geometry and Reality*, excited about that, a birthday gift from the cosmos, and I'd bought a digital watch, coming down on the plane to Grand Turk, staring at my odd new watch on the plane with its inaudible *tk tk tk tk tk*, feeling suicidally hungover. I wrote a poem called "Lucifer" about the trip, it starts like this.

> On my 30th birthday I got drunk
> In the scaffolding of that tower of Babel
> I'd planned to fuck god with my old gang
> Of mind assassins who did melt (from)
> I fell through frozen time to this parched island
> The beach night of eternal star
> Sea of possibility and infinite spacetime
> Mists on the Earth—What a laugh,
> To sell answers in paperback,
> When you see god
> Only piss to mark the spot.

Revising this with a pencil on a Turks and Caicos beach, trying to break through to some final authoritative vision of God. Ah, you can get the vision, you can buy it for $10 if you've never had acid yet, although it won't work the second time, and however you get there, you have to come back, that's always the thing, like Jagger sings in "Coming Down Again." Up and down, yah, surfing it, that's a big image for me, surfing the seas of life, not that I can actually surf, no, I roll and wallow in the waves. So we're down there in the islands, at Caldwell's house, he's with his wife and their two kids.

The thing I'm getting to here is the sentiment I mentioned back up the scroll a bit. Yes, you're going to die anyway. *But meanwhile…have some fun.* Which was from Doug Baffin, the Viet Vet, guider of skin-diving on Grand Turk Island. He took me out alone the first day, in shallow water around coral heads, and I got the picture. You can…really *breathe* underwater with the Darth Vader bobbler in yer teeth. *Snoooooook-phoo, blu, foo, blu, blu, bluu.* Bubbles dance up so pretty. Kick the fins, you're warm from the rubber wet-vest, you've got the weights to neutralize your buoyancy—all so well thought out! The big lesson, the major teaching of skin-diving is *breathe out on your way up.* If you don't breathe it all out, then the deep-water high-pressure air will expand and P*O*P your lungs to bluggy floo-floo spazz last horror-cough thub bleat. This is the Central Teaching of Skin-Diving. Breathe out on the way up, a lot a lot a lot.

OK, so then next day Caldwell comes along to go skin-diving with Baffin and me. A phrase Caldwell had fastened onto in the meantime was the phrase "wimpy macho." Which was something that Ace Weston had said to me at my 30th birthday party in Bernco, New York, Ace seeing me climb, handsomely, I thought, the long limb of our silver maple, like 100 feet up, man, me monkeying my way up there, so fast and practiced, meaning to impress the guests lounging on the lawn below, and Ace goes: "Oh god, wimpy macho!" So I'm telling this story to Caldwell down on Grand Turk, and he's overcome by the phrase, we're out in the boat, him and me and the Veet Vet guide and we suit up and put on weights, splash* splash** splash*** we're sinking, and here's the end of my "Lucifer" poem.

> Island time dilates and now
> I'm 120 feet down

In the gray blue brown invertebrate kingdom
The sun's a glint a shot away
My bubbles are like eyes like saucers
Satan's laughter sounds in my inner ear
Again
The guide swims deeper.

What's happening to me is "rapture of the depths," where, once you're deep enough, like eighty or ninety feet down, you get enough nitrogen in your blood to trip out, but nobody's told me about this, and I think it's just me. I'm tripped for true down there, gray deep, and crazy Caldwell is way down below me, a hundred twenty feet deep, he's tiny, further down the cliff. We're diving off the continental shelf, you dig, right out from the island, the shelf fucking drops off *wham*, like a mile straight down for sure for sure. Cool shit growing off the cliffs, big dick-like sponges, and blow-fish, barracuda, groupers, the whales out there sounding deep and deep. And Caldwell down there, waving me deeper, using the 'xact same gestures as a mechanic with flare lights beckoning in a plane, wave, wag, wave wave. I have big ear-pain confusion, I pinch my nose and blow to equalize the pressure *skkkkt-nnt-fll-skk-blaa*. Ears clear, I swim down to Caldwell. Thank god the guide comes after us, it's cold and I'm so confused up/down, the bubbles making funnier funniest noises—UP UP UP, signals the guide, we go up up up.

The high surface is visible again, wrinkle mirror moving…I couldn't see from way down there…up up, splash out, my head by the boat, take out my Darth Vader breathing tube, spit and blood. Blood in my mouth. I look over at Caldwell, he looks worried for sure for sure and the guide like laughs contemptuous, "I told you, Conrad." Me: "What? What's the blood?" Guide: "You got that air embolism." Which, *air embolism*, means I didn't breathe out enough.

I've gone and popped my lungs. Caldwell, a whinny of panic starting in his voice, "What can we do?" Guide: "Nothing *to* do. It's…" Caldwell: "Well, why are you laughing?" Guide: "He's only got a couple minutes left. Just…you know, have some fun."

I looked at the blank sky, the waves, the white boat. *So this is how it happens. It's not really so hard.*

But it was just the guide's war-crazed giggle, just a bloody nose, just…see what the kid can take. I was scared to breathe deep for a few days, but, in the end, had to thank the guy for giving me a teaching. Someday death just happens. And you're off the hook. Dead as a pair of polyester pants marked down at a K-Mart Blue Light Sale. "My fly sticks."

Leaving the islands, our plane shook it all to blur, the guys and gals waving bye, *zazz* back to Rochester, New York, and then to drive to Bernco, where we spent six years. It was like this: four years college, five years grad school, six years at Bernco State College, two years on a grant in Germany, two years at Langhorne Woman's College in Killeville, teaching math teaching math. I never understood calculus in college—there was no reason to understand it. By now I've taught calculus, god, how many times? Ten, twenty, thirty—eventually you learn the shit. There were no jobs at all when I finished at Rutgers and got my Ph.D. in Mathematical Logic. My thesis was like 200 pages long, and to this day I'm the only one who read it, and that only once or twice, god, who wants to solve that X-word puzzle. It was a horrible period, when I was finishing grad school and trying to find a spot as an academic mathematician, me grubbing up, at conferences, to "important" people nobody else has ever heard of before or since, just weirdos. At the last minute I landed a low-level teaching job at Geneseo State College, a guy from Rutgers was teaching there, my contact. And then, temporarily ensconced, I learned that it's like…if you're a professor they are paying you not to grow crops. Like some farm-biscuit crop-hop, the land-bank. "Eat our shit, boys, and don't do anything, and we'll promise you security and a substandard income till Kingdom Come. Unless we decide to fire you first." And maybe in the 2000's some of the by-then vacant dorms would be turned into old-age homes for the retired profs! Golden showers, enemas, light BM on Tuesday.

And then, just as I'd feared, they wouldn't give me tenure at Bernco, not even at Bernco. "Conrad, you'd be happier somewhere else." Like six years…that's the contractual term, the six years after which they have to (a) keep you forever or (b) give you the axe. I could hardly believe it, me the author of a book on the fourth dimension, my little *Geometry and Reality*. "Goodbye, Conrad. Someday you'll thank us for this." All my fruitless machinating, so futile against the blank fact of "Goodbye."

I lucked out and got that gig in Germany. It was a long-shot. And then the job teaching math at Langhorne College. And I lost that job, too, and I'm now alone in an abandoned building typing this scroll.

But…hey….Bernco, upstate, we had some real times there. Our third baby, Ida, was born nearby in a hospital in Warsaw, New York. They had a banner on the street which said: "WARSAW, HOME OF THE FOOTBALL!" Well, what does that mean? We never found out if (a), (b), or (c). On to the birth. A thunderstorm started as Audrey entered the transition between labor and delivery. I was standing by her bed and I could see out the window—brushy foothills leading to a steep hill in the middle distance, and lightning in the torn gray clouds. Oh, yes. What happens is that the baby is stuck inside, her face is turned wrong and Audrey pushing and pushing….there was something great, monumental, and noble in her masks of pain. Later she told me that each time she pushed she saw a yellow skull that came closer. Between pushes, the nurse would try to catch a fly that was buzzing around the delivery room. Outside the delivery room window was a plowed field and a state highway, cars swishing water spray. It was getting harder and harder, the doctor was going to use tongs on our baby's head, oh no, oh no. So I'm out in the waiting room after all those Lamaze classes. A BIBLE there with God's bad trip on all of us outside Eden, to Eve: "In pain you shall bring forth children," and to Adam: "In the sweat of your face you shall eat bread till you return to the ground." Fuck you, God, I think they might die, help me Jesus. Zen flash there in final despair: *Once you're born, the worst has already happened.* I'm taking this dictum to mean that, matter how badly this current scene might turn out, I'd already survived the worst thing of all, many years ago, that is, me being born into this difficult world—so I might as well relax. And in the end it was cool, here was Ida, a yellow-pink rosebud, unmarred, and dear Audrey coming to. In Audrey's arms, Ida opened her eyes and *saw* us, fully there in the new now. Miracle baby.

In college Audrey and I would lie in a certain field of weeds we called Estonia and she would brush my hair back off my forehead. "This is my darling Rad's forehead. Nobody sees it but me." *Rad* being short for *Conrad*. Ace Weston and I had made up the name "Estonia" for this spot, a hill in the woods near our dorm, the hillside covered with long yellow-pink dead grass-stalks, like sea oats. And sitting there you'd feel so pastoral, so European pastoral, imagining girls in native costumes, flowered dirndls and big red pom-poms on their heads, wooden rakes: Estonia.

Ace had a little radio—this was senior year at college now, and we were rooming together—his radio almost a joke, or a symbol of a radio, tiny, attached to a key-chain, and the only station it would pick up was some mongo clear-channel of a classical program, a single violin squee-deedling endlessly noodling sad and wee, in the grass of Estonia, the radio squeaking almost in pain from us squeezing it, drinking beer and then some booze we stole from another kid's room. We'd do room-checks, mid-morning, when all the others were at class, going through their closets for bottles. So this one time we're sitting in Estonia, Ace and I, with no Audrey, and some twelve-year-olds come to throw rocks at us, Ace calling out in a mechanical old-man voice, "Yer gonna get in trouble kids. You're gonna get in trouble." Golden light on the drops of whiskey, trading chugs, Ace's mind is gone, no spark of humanity left at all, my best friend is a meat robot. He wants to go swimming in a quarry nearby.

Robot-monster Ace trudging ahead of me through the darkening woods. I become anxious that in his black-out alcohol brain-death he will turn violent. I become paranoid, convinced he is planning for sure to kill me. So I get a big heavy branch and tip-toe closer behind him, ready to raise it up and… "Here's the quarry, Conrad. What are you doing with that stick?" "You were so drunk I thought maybe you were going to kill me." "No we've got important things to do. See this beer?" He fumbles an unopened bottle of Schmidt's out of his pants. Me: "What about it?" "I'm going to bury it here. And then I'll walk back to the dining-hall and get the Wop." The "Wop" being a beautiful girl from Italy, Ace being in love with her. Actually I don't know if she's beautiful or not, I was never able to tell her apart from two or three other similar-looking girls whom Ace also mooned over. "The Wop will come here with me and we'll swim and I'll fuck her and afterwards she and I will drink this bottle of Schmidt's together." Ace on all fours now, digging at the rank black muck at quarry's edge. His mind is gone again, and he digs there steadily for the whole time I'm paddling in the quarry. Later we make it to the dining-hall, I drop a tray of food on the floor and the dining-hall manager yells at me so hard that the cords in his neck stand out. I was glad to reveal him not as the good-guy he came on as, but as another fascist pig.

The end of senior year college was touched with that same tragic feeling I'd had leaving Louisville. I really didn't want to graduate. I'd picked some nice weeds from Estonia and put them in the double I shared with Ace, and Audrey would come sleep with me sometimes. Ace looked at the weeds and shook his head, "It's like Frankenstein trying to give a violet to a little girl." I had some yellow round-lensed shades. Ace was "Dog," and I was "Pig." We were finally neat. I'd painted words on the door of my room with water-colors.

> PIG'S DISCO
> Dance your head off
> Action Action Action
> All you can drink for all you own
> Do the Rooster
> Go-go Go-go.

Over my bed was glued a comic-book picture of Petunia Pig on a swing, her cute pink trotters showing with undie-frills out from under her skirt. We had a pile of bricks in the center of the room. Our name for the stack: The Temple Of The Barely Sub-Humans. A prism hung on a long rubber-cord from the ceiling to dangle over the bare-ly-sub-humans' ziggurat, and I had a Tensor light angled to split into colors in the prism. Ace and I had scavenged long three-inch-wide cardboard tubes from behind a rug-store, and had cut them to ceiling-height, and had wedged them into our room like random columns. We'd strung ribbons between them and had strewed fat polka-dot balloons. The enchanted forest, we called it, and I was The Magic Pig. Cooler and cooler. Me sitting there, staring at my wall. Like I said before, it's funny how a wall can look like a face. I still didn't have any answers, but I was finally having fun. I was in a good place there, respected by strangers and loved

45

by my friends. The sweetness of it, end of college, realizing that the hurdles were over, they really were going to let me get a degree, and a week after graduation I was going to marry Audrey. She was already at her parents' house in Geneva, getting ready for the wedding.

In the last week of senior year there, my college friends gave me a bachelor party. First we got drunk, of course, and chewed up a lot of No-Doz to keep going, Ace vomiting off the porch, but still swallowing beer and pills between… heaves. "It's frightening," says Ron Platek, "It's like watching a robot." Persistent theme with Ace. The porch was at the house of some of our other friends, Izzy Tuskman and Chuckie Golem, two five-foot guys, wrestling-team, from Long Island, Izzy already a good oil-painter, and Chuckie has a car. Wild little guys like R. Crumb snoids, they've rented this off-campus house with 3 other guys, they keep a motorcycle in the living-room, and *Sgt. Pepper's Lonely Hearts Club Band* is on the box, you dig. I want to tell about the bachelor party, but just a little more background on the house. Izzy had some poetry broadside, poems about fucking God in the ass or something, pasted up on the wall, a printed thing he'd gotten in the Village, I guess, and the big headline on this thing is FUCK HATE! And they actually got busted for that, the neighbor saw it and phoned a report to the Catholic League of Decency, and my friends had to go to court, all in coats and humble ties except Izzy Tuskman, of course, wild in his T-shirt, so far gone that there's not even any vague idea in his mind of how to begin to act normal. They had an ACLU lawyer beat the rap, so that was OK then, and even fun in retrospect. We all used to go over to the house and get high. One time we were jumping up and down together in the kitchen, and with the weed-stone time-dilation, you'd feel like at the peak of the jump you were just…hanging there, floating for a long time. This time we were jumping, Stu

Machotka, another good buddy in college, later to go to 'Nam, Stu was there and we were playing *Sgt. Pepper,* like I said, it had just come out. An unbelievable record at the time, a message from the media, "Everyone else is turning on, too! We're winning!" For some reason everybody except Stu goes and locks themselves in a closet to look at some stolen yellow traffic flashers. The closet has no handle on the inside, but that's cool, for Stu can always let us back out. So we're in there for awhile and it gets old, and we hammer on the door and no Stu. Ace in there with us has decided he needs a smoke and is fucking chain-smoking a pack of Luckies, *hack uhhh crash,* finally we splinter open the door and there's Stu, lying on the bed listening to "Lovely Rita" on the earphones. For me the Sixties really started in that house, it was '67 by then, and *Life* magazine had big color ads for LSD every month, it seemed like. It's funny how the establishment lackey media help hype these upheavals, I guess it sells some actual products on the side, like white go-go boots.

Anyway, at my bachelor party, there's a big cake, a single-layer job pieced together from several pans' worth, resting atop a turned-over cardboard box. Lettered on it: *Good-Bye Oinker, Hello Darling Rad!* Great. And then the box starts to shake, and out jumps…Sissa Taylor! She's a beautiful California girl with a great giggle and long straight brown hair and huge breasts and, being a Swarthmore student, a brilliant mind. Ah, Sissa. She's not naked inside my bachelor cake here, she's wearing a bikini and…*oh oh*, her toadlike boyfriend is lurking in the background. Well that's OK, for now a fellow Southern shy crackpot science guy, Whittset, comes up to me, bursting with news. Usually Whittset's idea of a good time is to do a lot of weed and go on the nod, lying on his bed listening to Cream and staring up at the ceiling—I'd spent a few afternoons doing that with him, the best part being a Victorian iron-work plate covering a missing lamp-fixture, this intricate shape painted white like the ceiling, you could stare up at it for hours and see faces in it, faces from heaven peering down at me and the somnolent Whittset. Anyway, at the bachelor party, Whittset sidles up to me with his thin-lipped crazed-yokel grin, "Conrad, we've got stag films, I rented them from the barber in the Ville, I have three of them and a projector upstairs." At this point I have never yet seen a stag film, right, and back then there was no chance of seeing the real thing in a legitimate cinema house, no chance of anything but a guy with a soft dick watching some cheesy blonde rub her tits. But these, Whittset assures me, are the real thing. At this time the draft for Viet Nam was getting real intense, and I'd had an actual fear that I'd die without ever seeing a stag film. At least by now I'd finally made love to a woman, losing my virginity with none other than Audrey, my bride-to-be, but that was *love*, and stag films were an important medium that needed to be investigated nonetheless. The best of the movies was one called *Girl Fun*. The next day I came back to that house, and Whittset and I watched it, with Ace, too, about 6 or 7 more times, although Izzy Tuskman by then was tense or bored and kept running in yelling, "The cops!"—wanting us to listen to his bullshit about art, probably, 'stead of lying there watching the movies, us boys all gristle-boned with pop-eyes, attentive as dogs beneath a dinner table. *Girl Fun*. The title is written by hand on a piece of cardboard you see, and then a woman's hand lifts it off and behind it is already a juicy snatch with real black'n'white hair. Two friendly women, slightly overweight, just soft-like, one with shades on, boy, and she licks the supine one's tits and gets down on her and then they interleave their legs and kind of bump and roll. They start laughing and fake a come. Almost like a religious experience, seeing those films, the holy mysteries. Sex is god.

After the bachelor party, my friends and I go over to another party, there's lots of parties around town, as it's almost graduation and we're the first hippies at Swarthmore, although we don't really know that, the concept is too new. We go over to the house of a professor who's giving a party for a student, Glassman, who lives there. Glassman, Bobby Glassman. What a guy. He was the quarterback of the football team that year, a philosophy major, and heavy into speed and tranquilizers. "They say smack is a gas," he'd muse. He was so strong he had muscles on top of his knee-caps. It was his sixth year of college—craftily he managed to keep missing the lacking course to top him up and out into workaday reality. He loved to get high, and get down, talking about heavy complex questions, the knower and the known, and always laughed when he saw me, "Conrad and his crocodile grin!" My friends and I used to marvel over Glassman, his magical charisma, and wonder how he did it. The main thing was that he seemed to be *enjoying* everything so much, like you'd buy him a hamburger and it would be, "Wow, you're buying me that? It's so…this is the best hamburger I ever had! Look how coarse they ground the meat…" Not really conning you, he was just totally into what happened. In retrospect, I guess it was maybe because he was stoned a lot more than any of the rest of us were, but even so, he wasn't nodding out like Whittset on his bed, he was running around and making things happen, and dating—my god!—the prettiest flat-face red-head girl I ever did see. So Glassman is living at some professor's, for free of course, and the prof is throwing a party for Bobby's friends. We get over there and Glassman is ecstatic to see me. I've never been friends with an athlete before and feel shy with admiration when I'm around him.

A few weeks earlier Ace and I had brought Glassman to our room with a visiting philosophy professor…from Australia…to get the red-face middle-age prof high. "Tell it as it is," as R. M. Nixon used to say. Of course we didn't really have any idea what we were doing, just trying to have loud fun, and it was a goof seeing the old guy try to assimilate it, peering at the Temple Of The Barely Sub-Humans: "This…enhances the effects?" Then a week later the visiting prof given an all-college lecture on freeing the younger generation, and the whole time leather-lunged Ace is in the back of the hall yelling, "Hey, freaky! Hey, freaky!"

At Glassman's party, Glassman takes me to his bedroom and gets out a little paper full of crystal methedrine. "You snort some of this, Conrad, and then a little water to dissolve it. Not too much, it's real strong." God. Then dancing with all the girls I'd loved from afar and not quite connected with these four fast years, and, to impress them, taking them back to Glassman's bedroom for a hit of "my" methedrine. Next day Glassman would complain, "No wonder you flipped out, I went to look at it, and there wasn't none of it left." Flipped out, yah, after going to bed in my dorm, I realize I can't sleep, my eyelids are like broken window shades, flap up all the time, and my heart feels like it's going to jump out of my chest, cardiac arrhythmia, I may die. I get up and walk up to the main campus, it's dawn, and some guys I've never seen before, even though they must be classmates, are driving a VW around the outside cinder-track. Very *Blow-Up*. Not knowing what else to do, I make my way to the room where the notorious "freshman heads" live. These guys, the envy of us "senior stomachs," are the new weirdos, just in from Ohio with all weird twitches and acid every week. I describe the nature of my drug-psychosis to them. They understandingly give me a handful of so-called vitamins which, on second thought, I'm scared to take. Eventually I come down anyway. You always do. And next time I see Glassman, I'm grubbing for more speed.

College ended fast. Graduation, and my parents taking my picture on what must have been the saddest day of my life. One of the top ten, anyway. But then came the big happy day, the day I married Audrey Hayes, June 24, 1967. I flew over there, to Geneva, where her parents lived in a modern apartment building. Audrey was doing so well in her New York grad school that Rutgers University was going to let me into their Math Ph.D. program just so that my wife-to-be could transfer there and grace their French program. French, french, god could Audrey kiss. I was in a kind of a dichotomous state at the end of college, Oinker/Darling-Rad, although to some extent the Oinker side made the Darling piquant. In any case, I was psyched to get married, the only one of my gang doing it, Mr. Big Weirdo not knowing what else to do, finally, but follow the traditional ingrained 50's life-plan: school, marry, job, baby. Looking back now, I see almost no one else who did it so traditionally, not the class-presidents, nor the insurance-salesmen, nor the jocks, nor the straights. But, hey, I loved Audrey and well...*now I'm out of college I'll get married.* That's kind of how I am. Plow the furrow. Do the next thing. What all's on the list?

Audrey's parents' high-rise was deluxe, with a swimming pool outdoors on the roof. A day or two before the wedding Audrey and I were up there alone and I managed to pull half her bikini off. "Greaser!" she shouted happily, dunking me, "Greaser!" My father the Episcopal minister did the ceremony, my brother Caldwell showed up from the islands to be best man—Audrey and I felt a little like the candy bride-and-groom dolls on top of the cake, me wearing horrible flesh-colored glasses I'd convinced myself were cool and the next big thing.

The morning of the wedding was a great scene. Caldwell, still single and with a taste for action, is sparking with this unaccompanied woman in the hotel room next to ours. She's traveling through Europe with her ten-year-old son from a burnt-out marriage. So Caldwell really has his eye on her, telling me about her the night before the wedding, wondering if he can climb across the hotel gingerbread to like press his white dong on her window. I don't want to hear about it, I'm worried, reading myself to sleep, reading William Burroughs's *The Soft Machine*. At breakfast next morning the wedding is coming right up. Audrey's father has it scheduled, for obscure reasons, at 12:12. So I go down to breakfast and Caldwell is already down there, sitting at a table with coffee and hot milk and the ten-year-old surly son of this woman he wants to prong. I'm eating, then suddenly Caldwell stands up clutching his stomach—he's always had a weak stomach.

He: "Oh, Conrad, I've really got the shits." Me: "So go to the bathroom. I don't want to hear about it, it's my wedding day." He: "It's too gross in these public European toilets, give me the key to our room, I left mine upstairs." Me: "Sure."

I get an egg and finish it, the ten-year-old staring at me fishily, time passes, still no Caldwell, and I go up and pound on the door of our room. It's time to get dressed in the rented funny clothes. Pound and pound, no answer. But I can hear rustling in there, Caldwell is in there, Caldwell is in there getting laid, is what I realize. So I run to squeal to my parents. My mother: "Disgusting!" My father, when I sock him the news, actually leans over like taking a blow to the heart. "That…that Caldwell. How…" I tag after my dad as he hurries upstairs to stand outside the locked door of my room. "Caldwell!" Sometimes Pop's voice kind of resonates with mucus in his throat, and this is one of those times. "Open the door, Caldwell!" Big scurry in there, and then Caldwell opens the door, bare-chested, and the woman is bent over an ironing-board with a hot iron in her practiced hands. "This lady was ironing my shirt for me."

Before the ceremony—remember that Pop is the minister and Caldwell is the best man—the three of us are in the sacristy, off the main altar-space there, and all so nervous we start giggling for a few mad seconds. It's like—we're tricking this nice girl into marrying one of us? Or, no, we're laughing from excitement, fear, joy. It was nice, it was nice being the wedding-dolls, and that night Audrey and I went to a good hotel, and I registered for us and gave my name, adding, "*Et ma femme.*" And my wife. And our honeymoon.

And then Audrey and I were in grad school at Rutgers. We lived in Highland Park, New Jersey. There was a whole routine, on Sunday mornings, of all the men going out for the *Times* and for bagels & lox. The counterman at the deli was sort of crazy, he had white hair and yelled a lot. His name was Yokl. He found out I was Southern and non-Jewish, and he'd make fun of me whenever I came in. "Here," he'd say, handing me my creamcheese, "You can eat this in *shul*." "I don't go to school any more." I didn't understand that *shul* means synagogue. When I'd come into the deli, Yokl would always know, it was like I gave off some kind of unclean vibe. I'd come in and he'd have his back to me, but I'd hear him moaning, his voice all high-pitched. And it would turn out that he'd be crooning, "Oh dem black-eyed peas."

Those newlywed days in Highland Park, Audrey and I used to watch "The Newlywed Game" on TV every week. We thought the show was funny, and it felt cozy to be doing newlywed. The host would always ask the guests a few questions that had sexual overtones. "When does your husband pay the most attention to you?" "When...when I'm on the toilet." We were both taking classes at Rutgers, which meant we had something to do with ourselves. And we were in love. It was wonderful. We learned how to make scrambled eggs, though it took much longer for us to figure out pork-chops. Fry, don't boil. Sometimes we'd do art projects together, like making a bunch of colored-paper collages to put up in the kitchen cabinets. A crazy old woman lived next door. She was bald, and she drank only bottled water. The bottles would be sitting out in the hall there with vulnerable foil caps. The woman at the other end of the hall often peeked out at us from her door, stealthily held slightly ajar. Our apartment had a Murphy bed, one of those beds that folds up into the wall. Once Stu Machotka came to see us with a girlfriend, and she soaked the bed's mattress with menstrual blood. Folded it back into the wall without telling us—I guess she was too embarrassed. When we eventually found it, we just flipped the mattress, it was okay, a rented apartment. Sometimes Audrey and I would sleep on that Murphy bed ourselves. Once, in particular, it was almost Christmas, and we had our own little tree with seashells and a tiny furry stuffed seal. We drank champagne and lay on the Murphy bed looking at our tree until we fell asleep.

One day I found a wrapped-up bundle in a trashcan right outside a jewelry store. I brought it home and gave it to Audrey, thinking it might be a piece of costume jewelry. When she unwrapped the string and cloth it turned out to be—*aaack*—a junky's works, an eye-dropper syringe and spoon. I threw the stuff down the garbage chute, then worried about the building manager finding it and getting my fingerprints off it. When I told Ace the story, he said I should have tried to get some left-over dried heroin out of the works. Talking big. The building manager was a genial problem-drinker with uniformly short white stubble all over his face and scalp, as if he ran a clipper over his whole head every few days. My parents were happy to have me married and they phoned up almost every day, just to get a hit of our newlywed energy. By then their marriage wasn't doing too well.

New Jersey can be more rural than you'd think. Sometimes Audrey and I went canoeing on an old canal. And there was a woodsy spot I liked to go near a railroad track not far from our apartment building.. I'd hang out there and look at the giant weedy plants. Somehow it seemed really interesting to be near plants, I could sort of hear them talking to me. Or giving off a hum.

When our first child Sorrel was born in 1969, no one else we knew had babies yet, and natural childbirth was unheard of—it was a weird aberration like eating brown rice. So, not knowing at all what to expect, we went into the hospital, Audrey huge and in pain, sharp intakes of breath. The nurses get her and knock her out and put me in the lobby with the old magazines that I read compulsively, frantically losing myself in the public lies, the false reality that's supposed to be so much realer than your wife having a baby. And then they wheel out the bed with Audrey, she's alive! And the nurse is holding baby Sorrel, our little yellow peach, sort of waxy looking, one eye open, and the bright eye fixes me, it seems, and her pinky (she has ten fingers!) waves. Wow! Do I get drunk now? What do I do? The rest of the day a sudden blank, go home and look out the window, the space and air, the reality of passing through another air-curtain, yet another reality level has arrived, another of the steps I know will come but never can believe they really will, and then *zow* Christmas is here, or I'm married, or…dead. The heavy earth on my coffin—*thud*.

But birth first! We bring Sorrel home, I feed her a bottle that first 3 am night, she wants one, we have a little bottle they gave us at the hospital, it's like a white bottle of ink, that small, and Sorrel baby is no bigger than a loaf of Pepperidge Farm white bread, on my forearm she rests, slurping in a disorganized newborn way at the bottle, and the moonlight comes in through the window behind me, spills silver over my shoulder and onto the white ink-bottle and the earnest round brow, *this is a real baby, this is our baby*. Life is going on, it never stops. I guess, during those graduate-school years, that's how I stopped worrying quite so much about death. I came to see that life is a process,

55

not an object. Does the fact that plants die in the fall mean the rose shouldn't bloom in June?

The strongest muscle on a new baby is the cheek. That's the one thing they have to be able to do right away: suck hard. So a newborn's cheek is about twice as thick as a grownup's. At first they don't even know how to cry right, the newborns, their crying is jerky, faint, disorganized. But then they learn. We had all kinds of devices for moving Sorrel around: a carriage, a back-pack, a chair and table on wheels, a folding playpen, a stroller, a car-seat, a carrier, a bassinet, a portable crib. It's like ants, if you turn over a big flat rock, you see the ants running for cover and each ant carrying a white larva in its jaws. The nurse at the hospital taught us the right way to wrap Sorrel in a receiving-blanket. Sort of like making stuffed cabbage. When Sorrel would try to kick free, her wrapped-up body would arch up like a…larva. When she *really* wanted to cry and scream, she'd arch so much that it was hard to hold her. Audrey and I would joke that the baby was "doing high C"—the C being both the body shape and the sound. Babies are one of the few things that always seem the same no matter where I'm at. Babies. Potential energy, silent exclamation points.

Audrey and I went to visit Audrey's parents in Geneva at least once a year. They have a very complete botanical garden in Geneva, near the big lake, and one of the gardeners must have been a head. Three separate patches of marijuana were growing there—it appeared as a "drug plant," a "medicinal plant," and as an "industrial plant." In the biggest patch, the plants were taller than me. Audrey took a picture of me standing with them. The next day I came back and picked a whole lot of it. There was no way to dry it openly—we were staying in her parents' apartment. So I hung it up on a coat hanger inside one of my shirts. In a few days it was dry enough. It was strange dope, always made me very confused. I mean it wasn't really fun to smoke it, sneaking around at my in-laws. Arguing about Viet Nam and the riots in the US. Maybe the pot plants were mad at me. I decided to bring an ounce or so back home through customs. I wanted to put the dope in Sorrel's diaper, but Audrey wouldn't let me. So I just put it in my coat pocket. At customs there was a big sign about smuggling drugs, and a trashcan right under the sign. Audrey was telling me, whispering, that I should throw the ounce in the big dangerous-drugs-trashcan before it was too late. But I figured that if I threw the dope in the trash can they'd arrest me anyway. I'd just be incriminating myself. Cops are like that. It's not like if you just own up, they'll forgive you. If you own up, it's a confession, is all. A man with a walkie-talkie was watching me from across the customs area, this is New York in August. The baby was crying. Another man with a walkie-talkie came up to me. Oh shit. "Do you have any liquor?" he asks. "No...*liquor*," I say, unable to control my voice. "OK, you can just go through," he says, glancing at the baby. "It's tough traveling with kids."

When Conrad Jr. was born, I was in the delivery room till the end. At the very first moment, he was sort of blue—from not having breathed yet—but his dick and balls were red. Ornament! His umbilical cord was curled like a phone-cord. He took a breath and started yelling, ringing right off the hook. I had an image of holding his mouth to my ear and hollering some Big Question back through all the cords to Eve, and the answer was "*La! Waah!*" I was so happy. When I got outside I shook hands with a policeman. "My wife just had a son!" "That's great!"

As a rule I was scared of policemen back then—it was very clear in the late Sixties what the sides were. It's weird now, writing this in 1983, that the ones who look like hippies in Killeville, Virginia, are actually country rednecks in pickups, the sons of the exact kinds of guys who the hippies were scared of. The sons of the guys who shot Peter Fonda in *Easy Rider*. Audrey and I used to go to D.C. for demonstrations against the war. I remember the real big one, the 1967 march on the Pentagon to "confront the warmakers." Audrey and I went with Ron Platek, my old Swarthmore roomie. I ran into trippy Bobby Glassman there, he said, "I'm looking for my Mom." Ron and I repeated the sage's dictum to each other, trying to tease out a deeper, more cryptic meaning. The Fugs were on a big flat-bed truck, chanting "Out, demon, out." They said they were going to levitate the Pentagon. It was a real fun time, football weather, and everyone looking at each other. Some serious acidheads among us, with bizarre paint on their faces. There were pigs on top of the Lincoln Memorial, taking everyone's picture with telephoto lenses. Walking on the bridge across the Potomac on our way to the Pentagon, we could look up and see soldiers with machine-guns in the open doors of helicopters. "This is how all the great massacres started," said Ron nervously. He knew, he was a history major. And when we got to the Pentagon there were soldiers with rifles, and confronting them didn't seem like such a great idea after all. But we survived. On the way back, Audrey, Ron and I sat down for awhile, watching the throng stream past, still coming, they'd been flowing in for hours and hours, the most people I ever saw. When I talked to my father that night he was upset about some minor violence he'd seen on TV. In his mind, it had been dangerous for Audrey and me at the demo. Turn off the tube and vote with your feet.

Audrey and I missed out on Woodstock because that was the exact week that Sorrel got born. But a month before that, we'd gone to Atlantic City to sit in a race-track stadium and see a lot of bands. Frank Zappa was there with the Mothers, but he was mad about something—some guy had jumped on the stage and shoved him—so all Frank said was, "This song is called King Kong." and they laced into a fifty-minute instrumental. Some people were sitting inside the huge speaker horns down by the stage, like, sitting with head stuck inside a speaker that delivered sound to the whole stadium. A whole lot of other people were underneath Frank's stage, smoking dope amidst the high-voltage music-power-lines. Janis Joplin was there too, screaming her guts out. I'd thought to bring the binoculars so I could look at her. But everyone around me kept asking to see too, so I didn't see that much. Just the mouth and anguish. In the parking lot, some guy was so tripped out that he was on all fours chewing at a tree. Classic move. No one went near him. Sea-life avoiding a crippled fish. In the stadium some of the guys were soldiers on leave. To fit in better, they were wearing long-hair wigs. One of them had a little sign he held in front of his chest: "Turn Me On." I didn't have any weed, and wished I'd thought of making myself a sign, too. I asked some smoking teenagers for a toke, and they acted like they didn't hear me. Nobody was very friendly. Sometimes I wondered if I was already middle-aged, pregnant wife and all, talking to my parents on the phone three times a week, just hopelessly missing out on the sex-drug-revolution and studying math, for god's sake, no hope of ever being an artist.

The math in graduate school was really hard, especially since I'd learned so little in college. They held our classes in beige concrete-block rooms, late afternoon, and it would get dark with us sitting there not understanding, dark and lonely and cold outside, sitting there trying to understand gibberish. Does life have to be this lame? I wondered. I phoned up Hank late one night to find out how his life was going, Hank from Louisville. "I never dreamed it would turn out so fucking poor," he told me, down for sure, old buddy. The more the media took over the hyping of the hippies, the less I felt like part of the scene. For a few months it had seemed like everything on Earth was going to change. Everyone high and seeing God—it was like we

59

thought a giant spaceship would come down and take us all to heaven. We had a new consciousness, it was supposed to be all different forever. But then the economy ran out of steam and everyone had to scuffle just to get by. If I'm so enlightened, why can't I get an interesting job?

Like I said, after graduate school at Rutgers, with two children born, I became an assistant math professor at the humdrum Bernco State College, a branch of the New York State University system, way upstate in a spot where it always snowed. After the first three months in Bernco, I was totally flipped, man. This was in November 1972, and I wrote a crazy letter to Ace. I still have the letter due to an embarrassing chain of mishaps, to wit, I had a teacher, my so-called thesis advisor who was at the Institute for Advanced Studies in Princeton. And I would laughingly refer to Ace's basement apartment in Gloucester as "The Institute for Retarded Study." It was a joke Ace started, actually. So one day when I was proctoring a test, I wrote Ace this letter, and addressed it to him as a "Dr." at the "Inst. Ret. Stud." And for some reason the Gloucester post office gave it to the Gloucester school system, who passed it on to the Bernco State college administration, and finally it turned up in my mail-box inside a Gloucester Schools envelope, obviously read and reread by every narc and oppressor up and down the East Coast. The letter, which is still kicking around among my papers, went like this:

> Dear Ace, I'm too paranoid to write right now—but I am anyway, so I'd best stop soon. I'm administering an hour exam to my Math 101 section. Just recovered from a laughing fit. Jesus Christ, Weston, I'm losing my mind here. You ever cop to the scrutiny a solid citizen is under? Functional paranoia, Ace—I got it bad. This afternoon I took a walk out of the town

into the snow-covered fields, a foot of snow. The fields form a checkerboard, half corn half blank, easily 400 yards by 400 yards per check. Warm day. I became aware of hitherto unrealized fact that I, like our friend the weasel, do not like to venture more than three body-lengths away from shelter. And for good reasons— "If I go out in the middle of that field some fascist pig will take me for a wild pig and shoot me in the head." Functional paranoia—how many "hunting accidents" do you read about each year? Now the way I finally got past this particular bummer was to stop whining to myself about the fascist pigs and accept the fact that insecurity is the price of freedom. You're unsafe when you leave the herd. And *then* I got off and merged into the One—well, almost. I was standing in a yoga trance position and viewing my body from the outside—this is possible, yes, I could even look behind my back and see which fingernails were dirty! I realized I was almost there—i.e. in a total union acid flash with the Cosmos. But then back came the hunter fantasies—"It'd be great to die so high." "Come on, shoot me. Now I'll die." "But, hey, I don't mean it, God." And, hung up, oscillating futilely, I got no further out. You gotta write me. I don't know what I am anymore—'cause I never talk to anyone. I would welcome advice on any topic. Heavy mind trips while proctoring here today. Dig it, my *now* is my future's nostalgia time. Merging into my surround, I see everything grow in size until the radiator in my classroom is a steam-smoke factory. I grow onward until I am (heaviest favorite fantasy) a galaxy. Love, Conrad.

You can imagine how many times I read and reread that letter, trying to decide if I had *given myself away*. I finally concluded, or at least hoped, that my note was so strange that the authorities simply did not know what to make of it at all.

My feeling of future nostalgia is a recurrent one, feeling the backward gaze of the eyes of my future self. It's usually hard to tell which particular events are being picked up as "stained-glass windows" of deep memory fixation—but occasionally, you can feel it. One of the strongest feelings like that I had recently was after we'd been at Bernco State a year, and it was time for our little Sorrel's third birthday party. August, the sun hot for once in upstate, me tying big balloons to the trees, filling up the wading pool, moving around in a happy trance, almost hearing my future typewriter getting it down, or trying to, the big yellow balloons with the red and blue polka-dots, just like the balloons I had in my dorm room senior year, me now in the role of a father, a parent like those big robot-people that had run all the birthday parties I'd been to as a boy, and my side-shift awareness of Sorrel's view of her first birthday party, her excited pigtails and yellow dress, the cake, the game my father used to run for us at the Louisville birthday parties: a saucer is placed underwater in a washtub, the children try to throw pennies so they land in the saucer. A bullseye wins a piece of bubble gum, a miss wins a piece of bubble gum, Fleers then, Bazooka for Sorrel. The little guests taking it all for granted—*this is life*, they think, *this is the way it is*. And after the long confusion of adolescence, I can agree, this *is* life, tying up balloons for a children's birthday party.

A lot of things helped advance my consciousness during my twenties—the new science I learned, being married and having children, and of course that big first acid trip in grad school. The peyote trip in college was really just… weird. I wasn't ready for the teachings, but when Sorrel was a year old I was finally ready to listen. It started with Ace Weston phoning me up. He sounded funny. He was staying at Chuckie's, about thirty miles away from Rutgers. Chuckie Golem from Swarthmore. Chuckie and Audrey and I were all at Rutgers then, and Ace was on leave from the Navy. He'd signed up for four years Navy after college, counting on them to make him a frogman, only not in Viet Nam. They found out about his college degree and made him a typist in San Diego. Chuckie's younger brother was dealing some drugs then and had a lot of acid around—he'd given Ace two hits of windowpane, one for Ace, one for me. So when Ace phones, he's so tripped-out that I can, like, look into the phone receiver and see his anxious face. The R. Crumb cartoon characters Mr. Natural and Flakey Foont are there with him, also Moby Dick the great white whale. A rough day for Ace, and that night he shows up at our place and hands me my hit of acid with the earnest injunction, "Don't take this, it's madness."

But a few days later is…Memorial Day, 1970. Not just any Memorial Day, but Memorial Day during the Veetnam war with rednecks holding flags in their teeth etc. So Audrey and Sorrel and I buy bagels and lox and go out in the woods for a picnic at which, it is understood, I will take my acid and have a nice time. Now, the spot I pick for the picnic is not one Audrey likes, it's in scrubby woods near the abandoned Camp Kilmer barracks, dead yellow grass and underbrush, completely isolated, but I figure it's fine. So there we are, and I swallow the tiny transparent chip. Wandering around, wondering if I'll feel anything, I look at my watch with its big sweep second hand and…I can't remember what these levers mean. The second hand stutters back and forth, not seeming to get anywhere.

"Conrad," calls Audrey, "There's a man over there!"

And yes, sure enough, here comes a huge hulking brute of a guy dressed in insignialess army fatigues with a giant hunting knife on his belt. He has a crewcut and looks crazed, half his teeth are missing. *Oh come on*, I'm thinking, *this is just too…* Like, my biggest worry of a giant drug freak-out has always been of being put under sudden intense world-pressure and being unable to cope, and snapping, or getting my guts cut out or… I look again, and the guy is really here, some nut who likes to play soldier in the woods alone and yes, we'll have that too, he's standing in front of me. A million brain-cells shrivel and die as I form a hard smile and say "Hi." The guy can't even talk right—I'm not making this up—he weighs 210 pounds, with a big knife, and he says, "What are you doing here? Nobody ever comes here but me." "Oh no," I'm saying, all quick chop-chop folding up our blanket, packing the lunch away. "We saw a whole bunch of people right over there, didn't we, Audrey." "Yes, yes that's right." "And now we're leaving." I say. "Yes we were just leaving," says Audrey, "Isn't it a nice day for a picnic." The big hippie-killer is kind of *duh-duh-duuuh* looking around for the other people we talked about. "It's dangerous for you to come here alone," he tells us. "Right!" I cry, throwing Sorrel into the car, getting her triple-joint folding stroller in the trunk—I hand Audrey the keys and whisper, "You drive, I'm losing it, just keep moving, keep moving."

And then we're in the car with our windows rolled up and doors locked, our big white Ford—unflamed as yet—pig-wallowing back and forth in the weeds by the road, turning around and *crash* the stroller in the trunk rolls to one side, then *crash*, to the other, I feel seasick, motion sick, teleporting to Galaxy Z and back in like three nanoseconds, *crash*. Oh god. So we go to where Audrey had said we should go in the first place, some nearby empty Rutgers playing fields, miles and miles of safe open space, flat green grass and I practically kiss the ground it's so flat and open and safe here, then *brrrrr* here comes a motorcycle, it's my friend Bert, a fellow math grad student, on his new 'sickle and seeing us, playfully drives right at me as if to run over my neck. I'm lying there, oh let it come down. "Conrad's on acid," Audrey explains to Bert. "That stuff'll fuck up your genes real bad," helpful Bert points out. Oh man just... let the colors flow, bubbles of them, as if all my nerves are transparent tubes full of Christmas colored water with tingle bubbles in them, showers of sparks and clouds of beauty, it feels so good at last, sink into that for awhile, then stand up, and I feel like a living part of a living world. Later, I'd put my impressions into a poem that I called "The Aether."

It is nice not to feel your body as a heap of rocks
a pile of concrete blocks,
sloan-kettering cancer research snippets,
odds and ends,
radio tubes
BUT RATHER
as a smooth foamy mass,
a breezy cloud of balloons
(tripping people feel the wind blow through them)
a ripple on the bosom of God's sea

Driving back to our apartment, Audrey is at the wheel, but I am driving. I can see with my eyes closed! Audrey just listens indulgently as I rave on about this, and baby Sorrel is asleep in my lap. I may be out of my gourd on acid, but it's still a lap as far as she's concerned.

The super-heavy-duty part of the trip comes in our apartment. I had a table all set for myself there, with typewriter and drawing paper and colored markers to "record my impressions." The gap is so vast, I can only laugh at these pathetic hopeful tools. And lie down on our bed to groove. The longer I stay still, the more the patterns build up, the weave of my jeans interferes with itself to make beautiful

65

light-purple moirés, three-dimensional patterns snaking like field-lines around the room, fantastically elastic with an ultrafine mesh, light-purple. The radio is on, Scott Muni the DJ with a secret tasty acid hiss in his voice, god-chords in the song he plays, if it is a song, unrecognizable 'cause it's so broke down to notes and individual waves. Audrey is off in another room, vacuuming. Closing my eyes I am a Tweety Bird in a cage watching her clean, I fly out and go into the machine, feather-fluff, a tunnel, growing light. Light all around me now, no space or time, just clear white light, and a voice. "I love you, Conrad, I'll always love you." It's God, talking to me, "I'm always here. Always." White light. That's when I really got over my fear of death, the light's behind it all—I saw.

I've been a mystic since then. Before that I'd certainly *wanted* to be a mystic, but I couldn't quite see how. I'd bought maybe twenty books on "How to Get Enlightened," and had studied them with varying degrees of attention, the least useful ones containing rigid and arduous programs of exercise, meditation and general life crackdown. The most useful ones were, I guess, the Zen ones, good old D. T. Suzuki, a favorite even from college years when I might get up, still half-drunk, and come out with some piece of gibberish and Ace chuckle, "*D. T.* Suzuki," as in *delirium tremens*. God knows I wanted to meditate, and empty my mind, and think a mantra, but…it gets so boring so fast. Why go to all that trouble when you can buy a hit of acid for $10? As the Maharishi once said, "I think it is very fitting that in America, the land of technology, God has come in the form of a pill." Not that it worked for everyone—I was primed for it, like, and the dose was the match to light the fire, rather than being the pile of twigs itself. Unlike mine, Ace's acid trip was a nightmare of self-loathing—"Someday I'll be a dead bum"—and for a couple of years we both felt bad about that: the 2 hits, and I'd gotten the good one and he'd gotten the bad one, hitchhiking brokenly back to his Navy steel bunk.

As for my mystical vision, I'd sort of discovered mysticism for myself back in high school, with vague notions of a "life force," or God, or the One, a drop of it in each of us, and when you die the drop slides back into the big God-pool of life, and your individual existence is gone, but there's a sense in which your life force is preserved. A different image of the same thing came to me much later, sitting with Audrey in an old graveyard in Maine, and the kids in the distance, and fishermen and tourists and everyone looking around—and the sudden feeling that each of us was an eye, a way for God to look at our world. A person is like one of those projecting eye-stalks that a snail sticks out, with all of the stalks moistly twitching and regarding each other—and there in the Maine graveyard, with the wind, the weathered stones, the sun on the ocean, I could, just for a second, feel myself not in *this* particular body or *that* one, but as part of a continuum of consciousness stretched all around. God is everywhere, and All is One.

I was excited about realizing all this, and I used to lecture about it to my math students, if any kind of opening presented itself. Hard to work this into a calculus course, but I did fit mysticism into a favorite course I regularly taught, "Foundations of Geometry." Even better was when I'd co-teach an interdepartmental course where no one knew exactly what to expect and I could just get up and rave on. I used to do this at Bernco with a prof friend of mine who taught philosophy. I remember one lecture in particular, where I reached the point of holding up a piece of wood, a two-by-four, and saying "This stick is as conscious as you or me." And meaning it. And as I would run on like that, the air would seem to get thick and yellow like it gets when you're high, and I'd feel like everyone listening was high as well, all of us aglow. Though, of course, a lot of people just thought I was full of shit—but, still, not as many as one might expect. It didn't really matter either way, in the end. Just...you know, have some fun.

After that first big acid trip, I never quite got so heavy a flash again—I think talking to God is a rite-of-passage thing you only receive once or twice in a lifetime. I used to be frustrated at this, trying to get back to the White Light, and still studying various enlightenment systems. A Zen way of looking at it is that you're always "in the White Light," always enlightened, even when, say, getting your picture taken for a driver's license. I used to try that on some of the students who'd seek me out at our house in Geneseo and ask for enlightenment. I'd go, "*Wham*, now you're enlightened." "No, I'm not." "Oh, well."

The six years of teaching at Bernco flow together—the main thing Audrey and I were doing was having children and raising them. First Sorrel, then Conrad, then Ida. Diapers, bottles, meals, tears. At work I was locked into the system, a cog in the education factory, going to meetings and trying to write technical papers on set theory: the mathematics of the infinite. Like I mentioned before, being a professor gave me a somewhat hopeless feeling—to have sold out so thoroughly, and for so little. When the college president told me I was fired, he had a box of tissues on his desk in case I started to cry. I sure wanted to, my six years of time there hitting a dead end. But instead I went home and started painting our house so we could sell it.

The next day, miracle time, I get a letter from a Germany, from the Alexander von Humboldt foundation, they would pay me to spend two years in Heidelberg doing research. I'd applied for the fellowship as a long shot—I was always applying for jobs, the whole time I was teaching as Bernco. Hundreds of job-applications, me always hounding old teachers who hardly knew me or who didn't like me, trying to get letters of reference, and endlessly retyping my curriculum vita, sending it out, sending it out. There was a special directory of jobs for mathematicians, and what you'd look for was a "tenure-track position" which meant that if you got the job you'd have a two-year contract, which would maybe be renewed and renewed until you got the *carrot*, that is, tenure, and after that you wouldn't have to publish or do student evaluations or go to faculty meetings, yeah. Some of the schools were run by such morons that they'd advertise, "tenure-tract position," reminding me vaguely of having a colostomy and shitting in a bag. Sending out hundreds of job letters and usually just a getting a xeroxed thing back, "Dear Applicant," and your vita all shit-stained from being used for ass-paper. And all this just to have a chance to make fourteen thousand dollars a year! But, hey, look how much vacation you get. For me the worst thing about teaching was to go to a departmental meeting. The sense of waste, sitting there in the basement of the math building at Bernco State, with two or three seasoned old parliamentarians debating whether to table a motion, or move to table, or table the motion to move. Once at a meeting of the Chevalier Literary Society in Louisville, fraternity-brother Whale brought in a rubber dog-poop-pile and put it on the floor, "Sir, there's a movement on the floor!" And, god, those math conferences I'd go to and never be able to understand a single paper that anyone delivered—well, maybe the first three or four minutes, but then the speaker would be off into his own mad, abstract coded-up brain-patterns—like who cares? I gave my own talks of course, and deemed them excellent, for sure for sure.

I remember a talk I was supposed to give at a big-deal logic conference at Oxford in England—this was in 1976 when we were still living in Bernco. I'd gotten an older logician to invite me to speak on my work. My work? I realized I really had nothing, but Audrey went ahead to Geneva to visit her parents, and she took the kids too, so that I could spend two weeks getting something together: "The One/Many Problem in the Foundations of Set Theory." My idea was to find something bigger than the biggest thing mathematicians usually talk about. Different levels of infinity, is what we study in set theory, and all the levels taken together make up a new level, and so on. Gearing up for this talk was my first time alone in years, two weeks with no family. Peace and bliss. I got a bunch of gone porno magazines—*Club* and *Hustler*—ate Steak-Umms, drank beer, got high. And, sure, worked on my paper, which wasn't coming together too well, and then it was time to fly to Geneva to meet Audrey and the kids.

It was an epic two weeks, alone in Bernco, hanging around at the Drop Inn Bar with a Viet Vet called Jimmy Fly. Fly was a few years younger than me, and he used to madden me by telling me I was an old middle-aged sell-out. He was unemployed, a poet. During those two weeks, most days I'd think about my paper for awhile, and then I'd go to the Drop Inn at four for my first beer, a big dark Schlitz draft, fizz tickle in my stomach. One day Jimmy walks in, "Hey, Conrad, you going to get me high or what?" "Don't yell about it." "Well, let's go."

So we go to my house, though I didn't really want to get high, I was feeling too paranoid that day, and knew for sure it would be bum. When we reached my house, I found I'd managed to leave my keys at the bar—subconscious evasion. We climbed in one of my windows anyway, got the weed, went back for my keys, got my car, drove a half-mile looking for a peaceful place to get high…and ran out of gas. "Now we can just go back to the Drop Inn," I said hopefully. Jimmy: "Well, I've got my truck there. We can still take a drive." So, dammit, we have to get in his truck and I'm sure we'll be busted, as Jimmy has a big Viet-Vet chip on his shoulder and is likely to get us in trouble. But—psychic power—his truck has a flat tire. I felt like I'd made it happen, and I was relaxed then. In control. We walked over to the college campus, deserted for the summer, and sat smoking weed on a hill to see the sun go down. There was a thunderstorm that night, and with my car finally gassed up I was driving around, out for beer maybe, and the little movie marquee read PSYCHIC PHENOMENA. Lit-up letters, and then the lightning started zazzing the power and everything would flicker on and off, me with this god-like feeling that I'm somehow pulling the wires on off on off, **YCH*C *HENOM**NA. I went in to see the movie then, and it was corny Boy-Scout-camp ghost stories.

Seemed like I always got really high when Jimmy Fly was around. Another time we were at a party smoking Thai-stick, standing on the porch, bugging some woman who was on a paranoia trip, "You all know each other and you're ganging up on me," she was saying, and out of the blue I say, "Well, you think you're cool cause you were in Kenya." And, yes, although this was just a shot in the dark, it was somehow correct, yes, she *had* been in Kenya. Hey, I felt like I knew everything, I felt like the Master of Space and Time, and then a different woman pipes up, "Can you help me, Conrad?" and I say, "Yes, ask me anything, I know all the answers," and she says, "Why doesn't Jimmy Fly like me?" *Because you're plain*, but that won't do. I staggered home in confusion. These kinds of power-fantasies weren't much help in finishing my aforementioned paper for Oxford, "The One/Many Problem in the Foundations of Set Theory," at least no help in any direct and obvious way, although of course the question of what it would be like to control reality is, in a sense, a type of One/Many problem, that is, how might the *oneness* of the universe fit in with the *manyness* of all us various reality controllers?

I finally got a start on some symbolic math ideas for the paper on the actual train from Geneva to Oxford, Audrey and I doing this leg of the trip together. They had a rubber blackboard in the Oxford conference room, on rollers so that you could write and roll the board higher and write some more, and then maybe roll it lower to see what you wrote before. In other words, a floppy rubber blackboard like in a horrible nightmare. I wrote up my stuff for a few minutes, nervous, madly ambitious, a clubfooted tight-rope-walker, and the grand old man who'd invited me says, "Stop, this can't go on. What you're saying is so obviously false and meaningless." *Well, hey, now...this...* "It makes sense," pipe up the Polish delegates—this was an international conference, and the Poles were into my work from my earlier papers—"Let Bunger continue!" So everyone is yelling, just like in the movies about Freud, and eventually I stumble to a close.

There was a drought in Oxford and all the ponds were empty. The rivers still worked though, so I did a Lewis Carroll routine and took my lovely Audrey-Alice punting through lacy, floating patches of an aquatic plant with tiny, green water-cress leaves. "Duckweed!" says Audrey, laughing, throwing a handful at me.

The math department chair at Bernco State College was a former Navy man. He liked to drink, and once at a party we got into a kind of argument. "You're stuck in the Sixties," he told me. "Yeah? Well, you're stuck in the Forties." It was in fact the Seventies then, a place where no one much wanted to be. "Conrad isn't Sixties," one of my friends told my boss, "He's Eighties." The friend was Audrey Kelly—same first name as my wife. This other Audrey was married to the resident poet of Bernco College, a big mean guy called Jack Kelly. Fat Jack. He was quite a boozer himself, and had a house out in the country. I admired him greatly—for his vicious tirades, for his poems, and for the facts that he was still married to his first wife and had three nice teenage daughters. My office was right down the hall from Jack's, English and Math being in the same building.

There weren't too many other people in that building who I could feel comfortable with, not that Jack was always one to make a visitor feel comfortable. Often, he'd just kind of look at you, and wait for you to leave. He was the first real writer I knew. Most of the other faculty didn't like him too well—many refused even to read his books of poems. "They think that because they know me, they know my poetry," Jack complained to me once. "They think I write fat drunken poetry." His poems were in fact quite thin and sober, lots of them about murder and torture. Jack's face would always light up when he talked about things like hangings and electrocutions. Yet, even so, there he was in a comfortable farmhouse with a nice family.

Jack took up cross-country skiing one winter, and got me interested in it too. In Bernco, it snows just about every single day from late November to early March, with an extra unseasonal blizzard or two at either end of the long winter. The snow gets deeper and deeper, and you can't really walk around in it. Cross-country skis were the perfect solution. The skis were like snowshoes, see, but with the bonus that occasionally you can glide for awhile. It wasn't so much that you'd go fast on them, but rather that, by using the skis, it became possible to go out into the woods even when the snow was three or four feet deep. And merge into the One. Jack had a special five-mile course he liked to ski, starting out from his front porch. One Sunday, Jack and I and our two Audreys all went skiing together, while his three daughters watched our three children at his house. It was beautiful outdoors, the sun bright and sparkling on the ice and snow. When we got back to the Jack's house, we sat down at the dining-table and ate and drank for six hours. What a feast! He'd paid his daughters to serve the food and drinks—and our kids were happy watching the old black and white *King Kong* movie on TV. With the good honest hunger of hard exertion, we grown-ups laced into the vittles, tossing down glass after glass of rose wine. But after six hours I was drunk, and I felt sad about it. No control. "I never went from feeling so good, to feeling so bad, so fast," I told Jack the next day. He didn't care.

My true best friend at Bernco State was a different English professor, Nick DeLong, a guy who came there a year after me. He, too, was a former hippie struggling for a way to make a living. I was cranking out a few math papers, and Nick doing some papers on film. Nick and his wife Jessie lived right across the street from Audrey and me…it was almost like a commune, with the endless shared meals, cases of beer, new records. Jessie was the most relaxed of any of us, a sort of pioneer woman who also loved shopping malls. Her cozy voice, sitting on our couch, the four of us getting high, and some babies crawling around, Zappa on the record player, and a blizzard outside, the colors of our living room dope-aglow. Nick and I would spend endless hours discussing our prospects of getting tenure. He was more high-strung than me, with stomach trouble and a real zest for departmental politics. He was a huge Bob Dylan fan, I remember us all watching Bob's *Hard Rain* TV special together—it was a revelation. Dylan never smiled, not once, during the whole show. What a guy! We four went up to see Bob when he came to play Rochester with his Rolling Thunder Review. There was one moment when Dylan and Joan Baez did "Blowin in the Wind" and lots of us were actually kneeling in the aisles, having crept up to get closer to the stage, and this included me, I'm a little ashamed to say. One night Nick and I stayed up late together. There was a blizzard raging outside, the wind sculpting the drifts into Martian curves, Nick and I standing on two heating grates in his house, overcome by the actual reality of the actual world around us. We really exist, this house exists, this is real! This was in the wake of a visit from Nick's younger brother, a skinny, engaging madman who'd periodically orbit in with his colorful life problems. Dennis DeLong, also known as Sta-Hi, and later the model for a character in my novel *Yes And No*, a tale about brain-eating robots.

Most of the time in Bernco I was still hoping to make some big discovery in the foundations of set theory, hoping to get tenure, hoping to be a full professor someday. And when it was suddenly over and we were exiled to Germany, I felt like a plant torn out by the roots. Nick and Jessie moved to Iowa at the same time. We four exchanged scores of letters about our anomie and sorrow at leaving the peaceful rut we'd had, our Bernco floating like a jellyfish in rural America.

But before getting into Germany, I've got more stories of visions in Bernco. A couple of times I got my college pal Stu Machotka to mail me bars of hashish, like a soft Hershey bar of the stuff, and I'd roll it into little pellets and smoke a few pellets or, very unwisely, eat them. The worst freak-out ever was one night eating hash, Audrey and the kids out of town again—on these rare occasions I was likely to try some special mammoth brain-torture on myself. This time it was eating too much hash, inspired by the first half of Baudelaire's *The Poem of Hashish*, and also by DeQuincey's *Confessions of an English Opium Eater*. I kept thinking I wasn't getting off, so nibbled more and more until...there was a big hiatus, all oriental carpet stuff, and I was in my body on the couch. I tried to stand up and fell down. Started crawling towards the telephone, thinking, "Call the police, I'm dying!" Thank god I didn't make it to the phone—*call the police*, indeed—no, I collapsed and just lay there. I had a sly feeling that this might be my chance to line up the sights and shoot through to the White Light again—Baudelaire talks about a "nostalgia for the infinite." But, just as I squeezed my brain through the concentric color rings, I sort of twitched, and I bounced back. Got up and went upstairs. Noise in the attic, squirrels, I knew it was squirrels, but it did sound so very much like witch's claws. I go into our bedroom, light spilling in from the streetlight onto our rumpled bed, and some trick of shadow makes BRAAAAAANNG alarm bells go off, and our bed is covered with blood, I've axe-murdered someone (*who? who?*) and I'd forgotten it, but now blood is all over and the prison escape bell is blasting BRAAAAAAAANG BRAAAAANNG, oh my head.

It was such a horrible bum trip that for a few weeks I carried a hand-written copy of the Lord's Prayer in my coat pocket like a crazy person. I was obsessed with the notion that if I tried to say the Prayer for help and if I said even one word wrong, then, far from bringing Jesus, the botched prayer would open up a dimensional door for Satan and his nasties. I was in a bad place that fall for sure for sure. I'd been reading a lot of H. P. Lovecraft, too, stories about young men who study the fourth dimension, heh, and a witch comes out of their attic to get them. *I* was studying the fourth dimension…and there were noises in *my* attic. I got so anxious that I even asked my father the minister to say an exorcism prayer the next time he came to our house—which had in fact been a "haunted house" for many years before Audrey and I bought it. The people who'd lived there had up and left one day, without explanation. One of the local ladies told me that these strange skippers had even left cereal in the breakfast bowls on the table, they hadn't bothered to pack, hardly, and year after year the cereal had sat there, dry and gray with kids daring each other to sneak in and eat a piece. Fear-of-the-devil and love-of-Jesus, two sides of the same coin. After a few weeks I got over it. It had just been a foolishly self-inflicted drug-psychosis. A mental adventure, something fresh to think about. Like going hunting in the jungle and seeing a rhino. To fully set things right, I nailed flattened tin cans over the holes in our eaves where the squirrels had been getting into the attic. No more creepy H. P. Lovecraft noise.

We went to the local Episcopal church fairly regularly, a forlorn congregation of, like, twenty members, me and Audrey and the kids there, taking what we could get. What could we get? Well, I liked the confession and the absolution, the odd gospel stories, the singing, and how, sometimes after the service, with everyone standing up, there'd be that same multi-eye feeling that we're all aspects of the One, fleeting thoughts in God's mind, snail eyestalks, dense patches in the universal fog. And after the communion, kneeling, it was easy to merge into the One, to feel there is a God who cares. It's handy to have a feeling that you know Jesus and God well enough to be able to pray to them—that can be a useful card up your sleeve in case your brain is falling out and there's imaginary blood on the sheets and BRAAAAANNG. Not that I normally *do* remember to pray if something really heavy is coming down. My feelings about religion are pretty variable. In high school I couldn't take the bullshit of the ceremony, the dressed-up straights, the sitting there. We die dead and forever, I figured, so why go to church? Basically I still believe that—I think selling religion on the basis of some putative reward after death is one of the loveliest cons around. Church give out nothing, people give in everything. "I'll pay you back in Eternity." But, again, it's process that counts. If going to church today makes you feel good today, then it's worth doing today. If not, don't. It's a non-issue, really.

Quite recently, like two days ago in real time, I was at my uncle's funeral. I made the mistake of doing a jay at the airport on the way down, and the trip took forever, agony sweat waiting in line. My father and my brother Caldwell met me at the airport in Jacksonville, Fla., near where my uncle would be buried. We drove from the airport to the funeral home for the viewing of the body. Before that, though, came buying some whiskey. "I need it," I'm telling my father and brother, "I came down here to have a good time, what is this shit, I bet you guys are already drunk." They kind of laugh, and we get, just to make it strange, a bottle of Georgia Moon, a legal-type moonshine that comes in the traditional mason jar, aged not more than 30 days, clear oily stuff. Caldwell and I take some hits, talking over old times, and then it's into the Funeral Home for the viewing and the Rosary. My old uncle is there in an open coffin, his hands on his chest, wearing a nice business suit, his eyes closed, but his glasses on. Later, Caldwell is talking about that, comparing it to the idea of an Indian getting buried with like a favorite tomahawk for the happy hunting ground. When you die you wear your glasses. Your wife's gotta get rid of those glasses staring at her off her dead husband's dresser. After the viewing, I asked Pop what he thought about seeing his dead brother. "He looked deader than hell." Not saying this as a joke, saying it sadly, almost bitterly.

Normally when you see a person lying down, you feel that if you bug them enough, they'll get up, no matter how tired or wiped-out they are. But you can shake and bother a corpse as much as possible, and the corpse will never get up. I could tell this from the way my uncle was lying there. No one has ever brought a dead person back to life. Ever. Although of course the priest at the funeral did whip out the Lazarus story, and then run it together with some crazed rap about how we have shared in Jesus's death so we're already dead in Him and are also reborn by drinking His blood and eating His flesh for He forgives us for killing Him and came to die so that we might live…what? I mean, if you ever listen to the number that the priests are laying down it's so utterly nonsensical. Christianity is clearly a belief system designed by many weird people—and this could be a reason for its longevity—the very fact that it is such gibberish means you can read any damn thing into it that you need to hear. And the symbols—the crucifix and the holy water and the wafer. Like a science-fiction religion.

All that aside, Pop had a chance to stand up and talk for awhile at the service, and he did a great job, very touching and eloquent, talking about how, when they were young, his brother would often get injured and they'd have to carry him home. And now...they were carrying him home again. Both Pop's brothers are dead now. Pop's not my enemy, he's my father. It was nice being around all the relatives, people with some wetware overlap, you can trust them, and fun to be together with Caldwell again, lying around our room drinking moonshine or pretending to be corpses, laughing like boys. What do you do about death? Just...you know, have some fun.

While Audrey and I were living at Bernco, we saw several Frank Zappa concerts in nearby Rochester. At one of them I first had my realization that life is like surfing. The waves of life surge up and down, ever changing, and you ride them as you can. Not a major insight, but at least a scrap. There aren't any giant final answers, as I'd once hoped. And, if you think about it, a final answer would be a terrible thing. Because the one question that the inescapable passage of time keeps posing is "Then what?" Suppose you think you've found some king-hell *final* answer, and you understand it, but... then what? You still have the rest of your life to live, you still have to make a living, you still have to get along with your family. We're stuck. No end to the surfing. Anyway— those Zappa concerts, everyone so high, and Frank so *on*, somehow picking up all our brain-vibes and feeding them back to us, even feeding vibes to the passed-out guy on the floor with a policeman doing the bug-a-corpse test to see if he'll ever move again. I remember a girl sitting in front of us with—this was rich—a pint of Old Crow in one hand, a joint in the other, and her friend is holding a little vial of 'bute that she sniffs, and she lolls back, "Oh, if her mother could see her now," says Audrey, in a merry Zappa-concert mood. And naturally I'm wondering how it would feel to loll back like that. One great Zappa routine, he conducts the band with idiosyncratic gestures—he pretends he's at a huge switchboard twiddling knobs and levers, as if the band were a single complex electronic instrument. And at the start of another concert, he comes out wearing giant-size joke sunglasses, and says, "Hey, can you help a brother out?" Someone yells something, and Frank looks down at his snakeskin pants, "*I* don't think they're so tight."

We saw all kinds of concerts in the Bernco days, Audrey and I. One of the greatest was the Rolling Stones in Buffalo, at the Memorial Auditorium in 1975. We couldn't get tickets, so I took a hundred dollars out of the bank and we drove to Buffalo in time for the concert. I shouted for tickets outside, and right off a girl comes up and sells us two for, like, a dollar more than the face-price—I think she was nervous about "scalping." The tickets were in the third row, but behind the stage. The girl was part of a Canadian bus-tour down to see the show. Uptight tour-people around us, really complaining when Audrey and I started dancing. Me: "You're *supposed* to stand up at a Stones concert." With the music so loud and the band so close, you couldn't tell—after awhile—what song they were playing, just the chords and the second-order resonances clashing and, next to the sound, or on top of it, the unamplified human voices of the Stones shouting to each other about when to cut in, or what was next. And then Mick, for one split second, was dancing with Audrey, who was the only one standing up in our row. And at the end of the encores, after it's all done, there's a tub full of ice and Heineken behind the amps, and Mick takes one, disappears, and I really want to run after him. Outside in the parking lot I talk to a guy, "It was a great concert." The guy nods his head, "It *mattered*."

We saw the Stones in Buffalo one more time, on the

Fourth of July, just before we left for Germany in 1978. It was like our farewell to America, and this time we had tickets in advance, although we ended up driving with a young printer whose friend had counterfeited hundreds of tickets. The printer and his hippie girlfriend. This time the concert was in a big concrete football stadium, kind of a nightmarish crowd, people hawking black beauties and PCP, "Nothing in here but chemicals! It's straight from New Jersey!" And then impossibly, there they were, coming out on stage, Mick and Keith and Charlie... I felt like crying almost, so glad to see my heroes again, the only world leaders I didn't want to kill.

Incredible jam in the parking lot outside afterwards, including a big bunch of guys, a gang sort of, homeowners with baseball bats and coolers of beer, I asked them for a beer—I was very thirsty—and they yelled at me and waved their fists. Apparently someone had torched a couple of suburban homes near the stadium after the last big concert, so the locals were up in arms. We're back in the car, my handpainted flame-mobile with the big red and blue tongues on both sides, waiting endlessly, but no sweat, I'm high, watching the whirl and twirl of colors. A young man in a hurry pulled up next to us, his whole car is full of smoke, he's puffing a reefer, "You all want some...*tea*?" "Tea to drink?" I ask, really really thirsty, not getting it. "No..." Pitying smile and a head shake, and he hurries off another way.

And then it was time for a garage sale to get rid of excess possessions so we could fit all our belongings down into a large-size U-Haul truck. That was it, the one U-Haul's worth that I would take to Louisville and store in my father & brother's factory. It was my father's factory originally, but my brother had taken it over. Pop was getting too old. I myself was uncomfortable at the factory, and scared of the workers. What did they make? Small wood parts. *Dimension Manufacturers* they called themselves—science-fictionally

81

enough. They'd make, like, a hundred thousand little cubes of wood of a specific size to glue into, say, the corners of drawers so as to fasten each drawer's bottom to its sides, drawers for cheapo dressers slapped together in Indiana. And now Audrey and I were going to sell our house, store our stuff in a spare warehouse at the plant, and go to Germany.

"Lumber magnate," my friend Izzy Tuskman used to call my father, but that was something of an exaggeration. By the time my brother took over, the company was almost bankrupt. And Caldwell had additional troubles, with a union trying to move in. The plant workers were non-union, making it cheaper to pay them, with fewer grievances and stoppages. The union—at least Pop and Caldwell looked at it this way—wanted to come in and line their own pockets at everyone else's expense. The men were better off without a union. Rrrright. In any case, like it or not, the decision on whether to unionize or not was up to the workers, and they were about to vote on it, and Caldwell was concerned that the union would win. There was one guy in particular pushing the union, he ran a shaper that planed rough boards into smooth ones. Missing a finger, as so many of the workers were. It wasn't a big factory, just a smallish building with yokels and machines. On the other side of the Ohio River, in Indiana. So Caldwell and the union organizer are understandably at odds with each other, and at some point the organizer gets so agitated that he decides to throw a punch at Caldwell, who's now the president of the company. Given that it's a small operation, Caldwell is on the floor a lot and now this guy is taking a swing at him. But Caldwell—my big brother!—is such a man, and such a weasel, that he figures "Let the guy hit me, and then I can fire him and get him arrested, too." And he stands there and takes the fucking punch, falls down, and the unionist is ready to kick Caldwell, but someone stops him, thank god, and Caldwell is lying there and—get this—picks up his head just a little, then lets it drop back down, repeat, repeat, acting for the witnesses like he can't even get up. So the unionist gets fired, also gets a suspended sentence from the court, and the men vote against having a union. Industry on parade. In any case, the plant had a warehouse with a section that Caldwell walled off for storing all of Audrey's and my stuff—all the paintings, rugs, couches, plates, books, records, appliances and personal effects.

Pulling the U-Haul out of our driveway in Bernco, I broke down for a minute, oh, our nice little white house, the big tree in back with the swing for the children, "I love you," I sobbed to the house, and vibrated off. To Germany.

I first visited Germany when I was about six, my mother was visiting her parents in Hanover, and she brought Caldwell and me along. My grandfather Conrad von Riemann had poor vision by then, and I was a bad eater. After every meal he would bring my plate up to touch his nose, so that he could see how I'd done. It was urgent to get me to eat, as I'd lost weight on the ship coming over, a tramp-steamer with robust meals that I wouldn't touch. A picky eater. It got to the point where I was lying in my bunk, almost too weak to stand, thinking, "Oh oh, I'm starving to death." Why did I do it? Hard to say—now I'll eat just about anything. On that ship journey, Caldwell and I used to play a game where one of us would be blinded by having a stocking-cap pulled down over his eyes, and the other one would give directions about which way to walk through the mazy corridors of the ship. We kept laughing and saying, "What if I told you turn right at the head of some stairs?" And finally I decided I'd better do it to Caldwell before he did it to me. The ship pitched just then, he lost his footing, and slid down the metal stairs on his stomach, banging his front teeth. I felt horrible. The teeth were wobbly for awhile, but then they got better. We made a lot of trouble. The toilet paper was too stiff, so I threw it out the bathroom porthole onto the deck. It rolled around in the wind and festooned everything. To find soft toilet paper, I snuck up to the captain's bathroom and left my turds there. They painted the ship's railings, fresh paint, and Caldwell and I climbed on them and messed up our clothes. It was an exciting journey. I feel like I've never remembered this stuff before. Where does it come from? In Germany that time, 1952, the war was still not so far in the past, and a lot of the buildings were just piles of pink bricks. You weren't supposed to climb on the bricks because there were still unexploded bombs under them. My grandmother had a big box of metal zoo animals, and a board with a picture of roads and cages. I played zoo in her dark hallway, and often we'd walk through the woods to the real zoo.

I came back to Germany alone when I was twelve. 1958. My parents felt I was doing badly in school and that I could use a year away from America. Why did they send me off like that? My grades were poor, C-level, although the aptitude tests said I could get A's. But for some reason I viewed myself as ungifted, not a smart kid. I had a terrible self-image. It seemed like all the other kids at the school had known each other before I got there. They picked on me a lot—not exactly vicious beatings, but…pokes and hard words. I once made a diagram of the class pecking order. The two mangiest chickens were me and a strange slobberer named "Skeeter." My mother tried to get me together with Skeeter a lot, since we "had so much in common," but I couldn't stand the kid. So I was an outcast in school those early years (which might explain why I've been kind of anti-establishment ever since), and I was getting bad grades, and I had asthma attacks.

My biggest asthma attack was the day I almost caught my parents fucking. I was out in the front yard playing with Muffin the dog and began to get that wheezy feeling. Like breathing through cigarette filters. So go try to open the seldom-used front door. But I can't get it open and I begin to pound on it, *I need my Asthma-Nefrin inhaler.* For some reason no one comes for ages, but finally my father appears—the house is dark and empty. He comes from the direction of the bedroom, he's flushed and rumpled and looks like he'd like to kill me. I know the look now, having given it to my own children on similar occasions. So my asthma attack escalates into a real blue-faced wheezer with my father having to drive me to the hospital for a shot of adrenaline. Another good reason to send me off to my grandmother for a year. "The air there is so much better."

The boarding-school my grandmother picked for me was in the south of Germany, the Black Forest, a little town known as something of a health spa. Königsfeld. Grandma helped me to start learning German by having me read a story about a girl who falls down to the bottom of a well and is in some kind of free-wish-land, and if she eats anything down there, she'll never be able to get out. All the grown-ups in Königsfeld called each other "Brother" and "Sister." They were members of some obscure religious sect, very Protestant. But they were good people, and I was happy at my boarding-school, glad to be away from my Louisville life. The school put me in with a group of children my own age or younger, which I liked, as up till now I'd always been the youngest in my class—for some reason I'd started Louisville grade school a year early. It was nice to be a normal kid with others the same age. And it wasn't boys-only. The school was very traditional European, with Latin every year, the boys sitting on one side of the classroom and the girls on the other. Stern old teachers and wild pranks.

Six years later, in 1964, I came back to that same school in Königsfeld as a counselor or group-leader for some of the little boys. The return was after my freshman year of college. I'd earned the price of a ticket by digging basements in a new housing project, and I flew over to (a) spend some time at the old school, (b) visit my new girl-friend Audrey, and (c) visit Caldwell in the Army there, stationed on the East German border. While working at that old boarding school, I even looked up my school-days Königsfeld crush, Renate. Her long blonde pigtails were gone and her skin had roughened. She was friendly, curious about me, matter of fact. But with my visit to Audrey coming up, I didn't get into trying to kiss her, although in retrospect I should have tried. Her family was nice to me—her father and brother were watchmakers, and the mother made big cakes. "*Nimm*," Renate would say, offering me more. "Take." On my days off from being a school counselor, I'd walk out and drink beer in the woods. Finally Caldwell came to pick me up in his tiny Fiat 500. The school gave me a severance pay of ten dollars. Caldwell and I drove down through the mountains to Italy, making frequent stops. One memorable day we got drunk on mineral water, driving over some high mountain pass, handing the liter of soda back and forth and roaring with joy. We hooked up with Audrey's family after a week, and followed her father to their chalet in Zermatt. Audrey was already there, and came down the street to meet me, her two hands tucked into her jeans pockets, her elbows out, her skin tan, "Hello, stranger." I held hands with her everywhere, even though Caldwell privately told me he considered it tacky to do so. Maybe he was jealous. Audrey was so beautiful and smart and cheerful. A prize.

Over the years I went back to Zermatt many times, and sometimes went out on all-day hikes alone. I remember a good one, where I started out early and got up on the flank of one of the two mountain ranges that define the valley which contains Zermatt at its head. I left the trail and headed straight up over the slidy shale, grabbing grass tufts, up, up, up. Thinking the whole time of the soul's ascent to God— well, really not thinking *at all* after awhile, just climbing in the splendid silence, the air growing clearer and cooler, and clouds of little butterflies all around. The butterflies like flying flowers, the flowers like rooted butterflies, the pale odors and far off sounds in the vast space-bowl of the valley at my back. The climb got harder and harder, dangerous even, but finally I'm up on the ridge, looking down at a trail with human ants on it, far, far below. "Shitty ants!" I'm contemptuous of them, so cautious on their paths. I lie to rest in the sun, and the air is so thin and clear that at some point I suddenly think...I've stopped breathing? I sit up with a jolt, it's late, I hurry down the other side of the ridge to an easy ant-trail back. On the way I pass a tiny, abandoned church not much bigger than an outhouse, which—it turns out—is what it's been used for not too long ago. I look in at the filth and mess, then look out at the spacy mountains, and the old truism hits me like a sledgehammer: "God's not only in churches. God is everywhere."

Back down in Zermatt, Audrey has spent an enervating day with her parents. One second I'm in the wilderness, then I go past some sheep and down an alley, and then, *wham*, it's a shopping-street, and Audrey is a little cranky. "Your fingernails are dirty." The next day she and I go out into the meadows together. Pale lavender flowers everywhere, like crocuses with long stems. I weave her a crown, threading one stem through the next, making slots with my thumbnail. She dons the circlet and smiles, happy and shy. An atavistic feeling, the two of us being lovers in the airy Alps.

Returning to my first time in Zermatt, on that trip with Caldwell, after Switzerland we two headed back into Germany in his Fiat. We were coming over a hill in some village and a woman pulls out in a car at the bottom of the hill. Looks up at us and freezes, blocking both lanes of the road. Caldwell hits the brakes, but his tiny clown car, instead of skidding, starts to hop like a stone on water, jump jump jump, and I'm desperately trying to remember an article I'd read years ago in *Reader's Digest* about how to survive an auto emergency. Too late, smash black, and there's a gap. Then I'm opening my eyes, I see broken glass and a woman's face, "Holy shit," I slowly say, and she begins to scream. I'd been thrown clear of the car and I was on the road right next to the woman's car, having broken her side window with my forehead. Here comes some WWII-concentration-camp-type doctor with blub lips and a little squeeze bottle of sulfa powder, he dusts my bleeding forehead, and a cut on Caldwell's scalp, no bones broken, although my knee is killing me. I'm brooding over that single dark moment of unconsciousness I've just had, and thinking how it could be extended, in principle, to eternity. Dead black nothing with no time left. I ride with Caldwell to a nearby US Army hospital for better care: stitches in our heads and penicillin. While I'm waiting, some soldiers start getting on my case. My hair is long (Beatles-style!) so they think I'm German, and they try to say insulting things to me in their few words of the mother-tongue. Seeing America from the outside there, the mean yokel aspect.

So after all these trips, it's not terribly inconceivable in 1978 that my family and I will spend two years in Germany. I fly over to Heidelberg alone to look for a place to live, me having U-Hauled our stuff to Louisville like I said. Horrible jet-lag nightmares in my Heidelberg hotel, all night hearing people at the door, my name in the street. Meanwhile Audrey and the three kids are waiting with her parents in Geneva. But then we're all together in a nice big apartment and I have an office in the Mathematics Institute of the University of Heidelberg. As it turned out, I'd gotten the grant on the strength of that dicey paper I'd presented at Oxford in 1976, "The One/Many Problem in the Foundations of Set Theory." In the end, I'd actually managed to put a bunch of solid math into it, and the head of the Mathematics Institute liked the sound of the work. The high-level buzz. Not that, once I show up, he's actually all that interested in talking about math details with me. His thing is more the getting of grants for mathematicians to come work in his building. So I'm left to my own devices. There was a certain problem I wanted to solve, the famous Cantor's Continuum Problem, which has to do with comparing the sizes of two different infinite sets. But it's a hard problem, it's a hundred years old, and you can break your brain for good on it. All fall I tried to prove some fresh mathematical results, but I was getting nowhere. The really frustrating thing about mathematics is that you can spend six months working on something, and have nothing at all to show for your work. Nobody's interested in an incorrect proof.

My mathematics research was frustrating, and to make things more dislocating, I was totally without marijuana for the first time in years. The whole two years in Germany I can't have gotten high more than two or three times, from stuff that old friends might mail me—such as a joint from my friend Sta-Hi inside a cassette of the Dr. DeMento Show. At first it made me desperate to be straight. Like, I'd be walking in the awesome woods and be thinking, "If only I could be high, I'd really enjoy this." But finally, grudgingly, I began enjoying my life anyway. Really, in a way, you're high all the time.

After a few months in Germany, Audrey's grandmother was dying in Budapest, and Audrey flew there to visit. While I was alone with the three kids—I guess it was for four or five days—I started writing a book which was in some respects about my life in Bernco, as well as being a science-fiction novel about the…Continuum Problem. *Mt. LSD 26* is what I called the book, thinking of my big acid vision in 1970 when I saw the white light. The fantastic element for *Mt. LSD 26* was a mountain higher than infinity, with God or the Absolute or the One on top. The mountain was an objective correlative for my studies in set theory so although, yes, the book was an SF novel, it did have some mathy things in it, and I could with a straight face tell the head of the Mathematics Institute that I was still working on set theory. Later I sent him the book—it was eventually published in English and even translated into German—but I don't think he ever read it.

I ended up spending most of my two years in Heidelberg doing science fiction instead of math—I wrote a bunch of stories, and another novel there as well, this one called *Yes And No*, about people transferring their minds into robots, and also about my father. And by the time I came back to the US, I'd pretty well decided to be a writer. Which came as a surprise to me. When I was in the third grade, a friend of my father's asked me what I wanted to be, and I said, "A businessman." Wanted to be like my father. But he was shocked at this, and urged me to be a scientist instead. Well, that was OK, too, but I took the wrong courses for being a physics major and I ended up in math, which isn't exactly science. Actually, in high school, what my friend Hank and I wanted most was to be Bowery bums. Maybe we'd get a degree in…philosophy, and *then* become Bowery bums. Use the philosophy so we'd have a lot to talk about.

Actually math involves philosophy as well, at least the kind of math that I do: set theory and mathematical logic. About infinity and, like, the shape of all shapes. A nice thing about math is that there's very little brute memorization. Everything follows logically, so that once you really understand a mathematical structure, it's almost impossible to forget it. I realized this after I started teaching math, although in college, yes, my math was mostly a muddle. As I mentioned before, math became clear to me in 1972, at the end of grad school. And I got my philosophical enlightenment then as well—a vision that shrinking and expanding are in some sense the same. Zero and infinity, everything and nothing, empty mind and cosmic mind.

As above, so below.

But now? Am I still enlightened? Somehow, over time, the whole set of issues changes. Instead of "Why should I be alive?" it becomes more a matter of "How can I *stay* alive?"—and this under increasingly disadvantageous conditions. I mean, sure, I hear "enlightenment" now, and I still I think, "Fine, I'll have some," but at the same time I'll be thinking about, like, how to make some money, and how to get along with my wife and children. Chuckie Golem and I used to joke about that—the way that such activities as, say, going to classes or meeting your in-laws are, under a certain stoned-out view, just meaningless uptight social games. But then if you push the idea, getting up in the morning is strictly for plastic people, and eating is, like, a pointless hangup, and breathing is way too much trouble… Burnt-out veterans of the acid wars. There's no way out, there's no magic key. "Love" we used to say. "Love is all you need." I guess if you had to go with anything, that would be the one. Love and a good pair of legs to stay up on that surfboard, sliding down the glassy sides of the manic-depression life-currents, running like hell to stay on top of the spinning wheel of fortune. The older you get, the faster the course becomes, nervous breakdown *whizzz* a coral head *zazzz* another fight—ahh, I don't know.

Reviewing my personal gerbil-wheel once again—I did four years college, five years grad school, six years Bernco, two years Germany, and then came the two years at Langhorne Woman's College here in Killeville, the only school to offer me a job. Langhorne is, a little weirdly for these times, a single-sex college, the idea being, they say, to give each individual woman a chance to excel in the absence of those hogging-the-limelight men. And there was a cloister-type element of wanting to dampen the partying of the wilder girls. I've only gotten two teaching job-offers in my life, and I took them both. Bernco and Langhorne.

As soon as the Langhorne math chairman and I met each other, I sensed it was a terrible mistake. A plump guy, younger than me, humorless, a square. He fired me after a year and a half. I was bitter and angry. I cheered myself with poem I called "Causes of Blindness."

> A champagne cork
> Exploding marijuana seed
> Viewing solar eclipses
> Staring at the sun on acid
> Breaking coke bottles with rocks
> Snowballs
> (Oh get it over with)
> Sharp sticks
> Firecrackers
> Oral sex with syphilitics
> Reading in dim light
> Living forever in the dark
> "Generation by generation the eyes migrate
>   upwards"
> Too much light forever in the dark

Teaching, so many years of teaching, feeling your fingers crumble bit by bit with the chalk dust, the chalk dust abrading you, rounding you off to a meekly lowered chrome-dome who really cares about trig functions. Soon after they told me I was fired at Langhorne College, there was a Faculty Show scheduled. February, 1982. My big chance to get even. Or to show who I really was, according to one version of "really." I started a punk rock band, the Dead Pigs. Another guy who'd lost his job, Tab Crash, was drummer. I was the singer and Crash on drums, we also had bass and lead guitar, and a horn-section: two saxes and a trombone. One of the saxes, Hondo Shock, was about my best buddy at the college. We often used to get high together and trash the language, or dance together at parties, the endless—and finally boring—little get-togethers of the same four or five "fun" couples on the faculty, the little nucleus, ah, it's like working in a coal mine and living in the factory town to be a smalltime academic, you see each other at work and at play. for the six months or so that we had our band, we'd rehearse every Friday. Tab and I and the others jamming at Hondo's house. I'd thought, at first, that I couldn't fake singing, but I learned how to do it. Not in good voice, not tuneful, for sure, really just a matter of…scream your song, yeah, puke your guts out, the pain and confusion, the fear of death, the coarseness, "*Uh Lou-ah Louah!*" Boy it was fun—the first thing I ever did in a group, never having even played sports, except for forced grade-school teams. The big performance at the Faculty Show was, in the band's estimation, a triumph. Maybe five hundred people there. We got through "Dead Pig," "Louie, Louie," and "Duke of Earl" before they rang the curtain down. I had some leather rock and roll pants from Germany, with leather jacket and shades to match, acting obscene and like rubbing my crotch or licking my hand, and the excited students at stage's edge reaching up, I could reach down and touch their hands, in the mass hysteria of the moment they were reaching up at me as if I were Mick himself, or Johnny Rotten. Whew! We kept playing all the rest of the spring, learned ten songs finally, but by the end of the year it was too much for all of us, too much life in the fast lane and then Tab and I were out to pasture, him out of town, me renting an office downtown to write in. To write this, *All the Visions.*

The old ladies who run, like, the offices of the registrar or the treasurer at Langhorne College still remember the Dead Pigs. The other day, I saw one of them, and she said, "I just loooved your band." "Well," I say, "it may not have been music, but it sure was art." "Oh, it was…*entertainment.*" For the big show, we had a real dead pig's head on stage.

Cooked for sanitary reasons. And by the time I came out, I was so charged into vicious-punk-mode that I kicked the head off the stage and into the audience, pig-brains a-wash.

> Daddy put me in the Langhorne pack,
> Bought me a horse and a Cadillac.
> I sold the car and bought me a brain,
> Now I'm half grown-up and I'm goin' insane.

For our last song, which was a doctored "Duke of Earl," we had a guy play chain-saw, a very spaced-out Virginia Gentleman, and you had to be *sure* he'd taken the chain off the saw. He stiff-legged staggered out with the saw and went for my crotch. I put the mike to the thing's engine while he revved it. Dead Pigs! I figured I wasn't going to be a teacher anymore, so I could do anything. When you act as outrageous as possible, 90% of people enjoy it—although the 10% who don't are usually in some way stationed above you. But, hey, I was already fired. Rabble-rousing, raising the public's consciousness. And at the end of that last semester I didn't even look at the finals. Extrapolated the grades from existing data. Rrright.

So now I write all the time, usually in my Killeville office here, renting this space in a junk-filled abandoned building. Looking out the window from my desk I see a sort of striped pattern. Scanning from bottom to top: the silver metal of the downstairs roof, green trash-trees, red and yellow buildings, a railroad track, factories with pigeons on top, more green, the river, a gravel factory, a cliff with trees on it, scattered cracker-box houses, a large institution for the mentally defective and brain-damaged, the sky. Sometimes writing gets me as high as I used to get from lecturing on God and the One and the Unreality of Time. Other times it's more a matter of puke your guts out. On the good days, it's like dreaming wide-awake. And a lot of it is craft.

I've written five novels now, and people who don't know me too well often ask, "Where do you get your ideas?" When they asked Isaac Newton how he'd gotten all his great new science ideas, he said, "By thinking about them constantly." Most of my good ideas come from no place, really, they just kind of pop out. It's like the Muse gives them to me. Also I pay close attention to daily life. Often I don't look like I'm paying attention, but really I am, and I pretty much remember everything that I ever hear or see. And I build things from all those memories, usually exaggerating this or that.

The writing makes the time pass, and some days I can get far enough ahead to take off, do a nice jay, get rid of the roach, and walk out in the Killeville streets, stoned and clean—that used to be a personal slogan in Bernco, *stoned and clean* for walks in those Bernco woods, always still paranoid and sure that a ranger would stop me, "What are you doing here?" You see people, especially teen-agers, sometimes so uptight that, as they do anything, like turn back in a movie line, they murmur out loud their answer to the eternal authoritarian question, "What are you doing?" Murmuring, poor kid: "…left my keys in the car…" I was like that in those Bernco woods, sitting in a hollow dead tree I loved, feeling like Bosch's *Saint Anthony*, but still with my story ready. Of course now I've lived in small-town Killeville three years, and I sort of embody my story. "I'm Conrad Bunger," is answer enough to the question of what I'm doing.

So, stoned and clean out from the office into the streets of Killeville, and nearby there's a street with big old houses, and then behind that is block upon block of black people's shacks. Not miserable shacks, mind you, these have laundry and shrubs, up and down the streets. I ride past on my bike, or walk past, and wonder and wonder about what they're thinking. If I actually say something they're always friendly enough, but there's such a feeling of alienation from each other…it's so hard to grasp that (a) black people are just like me, and/or (b) they're quite different. Although, finally, nothing hinges on whether or not I make up my mind or understand the people I see on the street, it's just…you know, have some fun. And come back to the office and write some more, and come home and love my family, sleep with my wife, play with my children, try not to get drunk too often, stretch it out, piece it together, keep life going that much longer, see God now and then, and postpone death. It's a life.

Take 2.

That's it? That's the best I can come up with after all these years of seeking Truth—*it's a life*? Come on, come on, all the left-out stories, all the unanswered questions—we've got to get to the bottom of this, right? The followers of that fat kid—Maharaj Ji—the cult called the Divine Light Mission, when one of their members turned out to be a spy for the IRS, they took him to a garage and sat him in a chair and told him he was going to "receive Truth." And then hit him over the head with a hammer, really hard. So now if, in a city, I see some wastrel leaning out a window vomiting, I like to say, "He's receiving Truth." Mocking my own quest a little bit. But surely life is more than staying alive.

Life is about trying to become immortal, in a way. Two kinds of immortality: having children, being an artist. Your children are, after all, very much like you. Watching mine grub around and read comics and be happy, I think my own childhood is, in a sense, not lost. Those happy childhood hazy days, before you noticed time is moving. I'm not there anymore, but the kids are. It's like the Ages of Man are constants, roles in an endless play, with ever new actors. Romeo still lives, childhood too. And there's no absolute need that the immortality-granting new children be your own. In the random shuffling of genetic yeses and noes, you'd expect anyway there to be always kids more or less like you were. Racial immortality.

And what about that artistic immortality? You can view the body and brain as hardware—wet, organic hardware—and the ideas, the attitudes, the memories—they're software. So I hand you my software on a scroll, you program it into yourself and you become me, right? That's what this book is for, you understand, *All the Visions*. You see me, you be me. Like, leaving a movie, say the old *Breathless* with Belmondo, you are him, there in the traffic, if a cop comes up you'll blow him away, right. Or after reading Henry Miller you want food and sex, more gusto, baby. As long as an artist's program is running in your head, *you are that artist*. Twinking, I call it, a made-up word. Verb or noun. To twink someone; to be a twink. I've learned most of my stuff by twinking people.

I twinked Jack Kerouac in high school and college, studying his writings, trying to think and act just like him. He's got a good, strong rap but…when you're getting to be about 40, and you start looking at how Jack drank himself to death, you think: "Time for a new role-model." Twink someone else, already. I flashed that realization for sure last fall, eight months ago. It was Halloween and I'd gone more or less nuts, horrible fights with Audrey, me on the verge of divorce, suicide, madness and had to like leave town. I got a plane up to Ace's—he has a used-book-store in Gloucester (anagram = *Glue Corset*), and, while talking things over with him, I realized, "Hey, I don't have to destroy myself just to prove that I'm a real writer." Or to prove I'm not really a sold-out middle-aged asshole. My band The Dead Pigs had gotten together one last time for that Halloween concert, Tab Crash back in town, and I painted half my face black with poster paint, the lower half, and sprinkled glitter on the paint while it was wet, also a black glitter-dot in the center of my forehead. There were two new young guitarists, who looked at me in doubt, "I don't believe you." But we got in a groove on the Jerry Lee Lewis song, "Whole Lotta Shakin," and did a version that lasted ninety minutes, just that one song, plenty of time for background rant and rave, smash bottles in front of the stage, shove a guy who tried to grab the mike. Walking over to the gig I was so amped that the time-flow was funny and I almost got run over crossing the street. Then come back home and have another fight with Audrey, we'd been fighting for six months over some marriage problems, and I lose it totally and get out the old stag-horn-handled carving knife that Pop would use on our happy Sunday Louisville roast beef. I'm not threatening Audrey with it, no I'm threatening to stab myself in the heart with the beautiful antique father-knife I was so proud to own, how pathetic. Too much scary drama. A drunk with a knife. Audrey wanted me out of the house.

The next day I flew to Gloucester, and Ace Weston took me in. Insanely I brought my heavy rose-red Selectric typewriter in my suitcase, also Clash and Ramones records. I saw myself as Rocky visiting his wise old trainer, walking in the woods near the Gloucester ocean, me outlining a whole great plan for a book or thought-pattern, and then forgetting it and asking Ace what I'd just said. He shakes his head sadly. "Can't remember? That's the marijuana." While I was up there, sitting in at Ace's store for him while he made his real money painting stores and offices, I typed an SF story about a man who shoots his wife, but then it turns out that her body was a robot copy and she had used space-distortion to hide inside the skull-space of that robot body, and she climbs out unharmed, expanding back to normal, but meanwhile the husband has piloted his space-ship toward a small black hole, but instead of being eaten up, he's got the little black hole stuck inside the middle of his head so that now there's an infinite skull-space for his gamma-radiated brain cells to grow into. Me imagining that somehow this hairball story made things right. *Ugh.* When I got home, I got real—I tried a lot harder with Audrey, and slowly things got better. So much for being Jack K.—not that I've truly given up on that, sitting here and typing on my rolly scroll.

And I've twinked who else besides Jack? Oh, Einstein for sure, that's where I got started on writing, trying to explain his theory of relativity. At Bernco State I always taught my special course "Foundations of Geometry," which no one else wanted to teach. I made it be a course about the fourth dimension: how it can be used to make time seem static, how it can be used to understand curved space, how it can lead to parallel universes, and how it can be used to view each of us mortals as a part of a single trans-spatial whole. And there wasn't any book on all these topics, although I'd sought one for a long time, so I wrote my own book for the course, my *Geometry and Reality*, first distributing it in mimeographed form, and then, over the semesters, honing it to the point where it appeared as a paperback from an off-beat little publisher in New York. Why a whole book? Well, like I'm saying, there's several kinds of fourth dimension besides the geometric notion of a direction totally different from any direction we can point to. I found pieces of the 4D puzzle scattered across a wide range of books, some of the best being those by Sir Arthur Eddington (*twink*), the greatest popular-science-writer who ever lived.

Once I saw a little picture of Eddington and Einstein in the newspaper, Einstein is mellow, as always, with his white 'stache and big wrinkled forehead, and Eddington looks, poor guy, like an excited light-bulb. Another great picture of Einstein—*two* more great pictures, actually—the one is Einstein in a level-brim leather hat and a leather trench-coat, calm as always, staring out at the camera without even a mustache, and next to him is Steinmetz, the wizard who started General Electric, Steinmetz a hunchback, his upper body is slid way to one side, he's holding a big cigar and staring out, he's as gone as the big E. The other picture is in color, from a German magazine, it's Einstein and Kurt Gödel (*twink*), who was a famous logician, a refugee of WWII who found peace at the Institute of Advanced Study in Princeton as did Einstein. Gödel was quite a bit younger than Einstein, you can sort of see that in the picture, Kurt with shoe-polish black-leather hair and a kind of double-breasted big-lapel zoot-suit, Einstein in some fucking sweatshirt, the usual expression, his arm around young Kurt—who suffered at the time from periodic bouts of severe depression, almost to the point of nuthouse. Einstein cheered Gödel up by teaching him the General Theory of Relativity—I love it—and then Gödel used what he'd learned to write a paper, "A remark on the Relationship Between Relativity Theory and Idealistic Philosophy," where he proved that it would be in principle possible for our universe to allow time-travel. And thus G had demonstrated that the past may still exist, and the future may already exist, and that all spacetime can exist as a whole, with real passage of time, so that death, you dig, is really not something that *happens*, you are just, like, such-and-so big of a region of spacetime, and you will always be there. In eternity. I think I mentioned this before. As Meister Eckhart says, "The Creation is not some distant event, the Creation is happening now."

After awhile, I was heavier into twinking Gödel than Einstein. I read all the papers that G wrote, and some of them are really hard, I mean to tell you. I don't think I could climb all those peaks anymore, but as a madly ambitious young club-footed tight-rope-walker, hoping to break the bank of the Absolute, *despite my deformities*, I read and read them. One of Gödel's shorter papers, "Remarks Before the Princeton Bicentennial Conference on Mathematics," written in 1946, the year I was born, and dealing with notions of mathematical definability—I must have read this paper fifty times or a hundred, and eventually I wrote my Ph. D. thesis about its ideas. Joy of joys, I in fact got to meet Gödel at the Institute for Advanced Study in Princeton, and talked to him a few times. Meeting him was a huge thing for me. At the time of meeting G, I was very hung-up on the dream of getting into the Institute for Advanced Study after graduate school, and I hoped the contact would help. I was at Rutgers, about thirty miles from Princeton, and the teacher I was doing my thesis with was spending a year at the Institute. They don't have classes at the Institute, just permanent guys (Faculty) and visiting guys (Fellows). My advisor was a very strange man, a human skeleton, he had some kind of disease as a result of a motorcycle accident (he claimed) and had to like stand up in stages, first his ass and then his torso. It might have been that he was anorexic. Anyway, he got me into a seminar at the Institute with a Japanese mathematician, Gaisi Takeuti, a really great guy who, for a time, I mentally blended with the Zen-sage D. T. Suzuki. Though, finally when I asked Takeuti what he thought of Zen, he said, "Oh, very boring to meditate. Almost worse than praying." And of course he adds the mandatory Zen remark, "I know nothing about Zen." And being in with these guys, I finally get to meet King Kurt in his office, which was just great, the smartest man I ever spoke to. Though also, seeing him, and realizing that he was old and almost dead, there was a feeling of—*this only goes so far*. In 1975, I wrote a poem along these lines, "Kurt Gödel."

> I phoned him the other day,
> And we talked about Set Theory,
> He proved the big theorems during the Depression.
>
> He gave me a shot of the old-time religion,
> "You should do *real* mathematics,

The true scientist must believe in the Absolute."

"One pushes upwards into an empty city" is what
The *I Ching* had remarked when
Urging me to call him.

After the call I went outside and
Wondered what to do in the empty city—
Real mathematics does not apply to the world.
But which is empty?

A few years later, in 1978, and I was working at Bernco, never having gotten into the Institute, Kurt Gödel died. It was the same day that Hubert Humphrey died, just like Aldous Huxley dying on the day JFK got shot. I wrote some reminiscences of G for a magazine called *Science 82* and I got $1500 for that. I felt a little cheap or opportunistic doing that, like Judas with his silver, but in the end, that little article served as a seed for my maximum-effort non-fiction tome, *Infinity And How To Get There*, a book that King Kurt might have liked.

For me, a big thing about Einstein and Gödel was that both were pretty well known to be heavy into mysticism. What is mysticism? Three teachings. I gave a talk on it here in Killeville last fall for a woman poet friend, Sondra Tupperware, who held a mock graduation in honor of quitting night-school, a great ceremony with even my father there to give the benediction, and, at the end, we sang the classic anarchist song: "Take Me Out to the Ball-Game." The three central teachings of mysticism: (1) All is One, (2) The One is Unknowable, (3) The One is Right Here.

All is One, that's when you feel like you're part of everything around you, the wind blows through you, patterns in the jelly. I had a good rush of that feeling in Germany, high on life, right outside the Deutsche Bank, I think I was almost through writing my novel *Mt. LSD 26*, or maybe I'd started on my next novel, *Yes And No*. Anyway, there was a lovely frozen moment outside the bank there, with the traffic whizzing past, the Heidelberg citizens moving along, and I saw things as *trails in the air*, spacetime trails. A feeling that in fact we're patterns moving past each other—but all in lovely celestial harmony. There was a photo of a woman in the window of that bank, she had a smile like a 50's Detroit car-grill, her teeth big and white, I used to think about that woman a lot. German women—hey, the Germans are not in fact fat. They don't eat lunch or breakfast or something, or maybe it's the lack of junk food. Trim, tan, the frank way that some women would look at me on the tram-line in to my office…whew! But I always ended up at my desk at the Mathematics Institute. It was a great building, modern but with nothing flimsy about it. Solid and utterly quiet. I spent months there, thoroughly twinking Georg Cantor, who invented infinite numbers. I read all his philosophical essays on God and Infinity, they're untranslated, so I had to read them in German, which felt scholarly and far-out. Cantor, another scientist driven into mysticism, and this carried over into my novel about infinity, *Mt. LSD 26*.

On the street, "mysticism" means, to the average person, "bullshit." When my *Mt. LSD 26* was eventually published as a science-fiction paperback, they referred to the inspirational book *Jonathan Livingston Seagull* on my cover, that being a book I'd never read, although I did read a parody of it called *Jonathan Segal Chicken*, a slim volume of which, when I showed it to Ace, he said, "Do you realize what total contempt that parody-title expresses? Like, why not *Jonathan Bullshit Blowjob*?" Dig it. Jonathan Bullshit Blowjob for sure. But, like I'm telling you, there's really just three simple mystic teachings. I got another drug-free flash of *All is One* in grad school, waiting for Audrey outside the building where she took her French classes, watching the birds nest in the ivy on a red-brick wall, the sun slanting down just so, lit wall, unlit wall, light pink, dark pink, here I am. In the world. Part of it. All is One.

Back onto the topic of drug-free visions, at Rutgers I became friends with Stu Machotka's younger brother Eddie, and some years later, when Eddie had grown to wisdom, I wrote him a letter asking, "Is there any hope of staying high without drugs?" His answer: "Conrad, you can make it without drugs. But not in *this* world." Eddie started Rutgers as a freshman just as I started my first year of graduate study in mathematics there. When I first saw Eddie, he was wearing the same shades that Stu wore during freshman year. And I had a memory flash of Stu way back then wearing those shades and teaching me to play Frisbee and explaining about the mezuzah he wore around his neck. And now four years later it's Eddie there in front of me, looking the same as Stu, and I realize college is really over for me, here's a new generation, a new set, starting it all over. I was kind of broken-hearted—I'd liked college so much, and was upset also to see myself another step closer to the urinal. I went home and put my face in Audrey's lap and bawled, then said, "Well, if we're getting so old, Audrey, we might as well have something to show for it. Let's have a baby." She was up for the idea.

As newlyweds there at Rutgers, living in Highland Park, N.J., Audrey and I both in graduate-school, we "took Eddie under our wing," and had him over for dinner often, sometimes with his no-good roommate who started out the year a fat wise-ass from Long Island, but ended the year thin and yellow as a wheat-straw-paper joint. Eddie took to drugs like a duck to water, and after two years he was really losing it. I ran into him in the college bookstore—I went there a lot, shoplifting a few titles a week by the "purloined letter" method, i.e. I'd walk out with the book I wanted in my hand. Ran into Eddie there and he's…in tears, telling me about how the Rolling Stones killed Sharon Tate, and the Beatles knew it was going to happen, "Here, Conrad, look on this cover of *Abbey Road*, you see how Paul is the corpse and Ringo is the gravedigger and George is the minister and John is God. And see…way back there in the picture, those three people, that's Sharon Tate and Abby Folger and…they've *won*, don't you understand, and the others are *losing*, it's just so…" "You've been taking too much acid, Eddie." He dropped out of Rutgers soon after that, though we still kept seeing him, still do.

Let's see, I'm, uh, talking about those three central teachings, yeah. The second one is, *The One is Unknowable*. The idea is that there's no completely accurate way to describe the One, the Void, God, the Absolute, the Cosmos, what-you-see-when-you-come, or a good ripe fart…the fart vision came to me the second time I took acid, the first of the acid trips being in grad school, like I already told about, and the second being while a pathetic peon grubber at Bernco State College. A really depressing trip that second one. My louche mathematician friend Bugs had mailed me the dose inside a gospel-tract comic book; he'd pasted it into the "No" box on the last page where they asked if I accepted Jesus Christ as my own personal Savior. Anyway, if the first trip had shown me the One, the second showed me the Many. I got out of my body okay, leaving it on the living room couch, with the roses on the rug a-billow, got out and headed for the White Light, high atop Mt. LSD 26. But when I got to where I thought I'd find the Light, there was just a gazebo, like in a city park with trampled grass, and some Chicanos hanging around. "Hey, man, you see God today?" "I no see Him yet." Beercans, broken dreams. Later that same night I saw the invention of language, and I got a peep into my future—I saw this scroll-book I'm writing here, for instance—and then baby Conrad Jr. woke up and needed his bottle, the whole bed is latex and milk as I feed him, then he's asleep, my son, I tuck him in into his crib, I lie down on the spare bed in his room so as not to disturb Audrey with my fretful flailing, and I see a nasty vision of myself as some feeble bumbler, like building airplanes that never fly and sticking out my tongue going *yabba-gabba* with spit-streamers, and locked up in a nuthouse where you belong. And then around dawn, two clear messages: (1) Shave off your mustache, and (2) Everything they do down at Bernco State is farting. Vision of a fat colleague lifting up a wide cheek and getting off a mellow one. *Pppooooott!* The classification of farts that my father taught me: "Conrad, there are three kinds of farts: (a) the string of pearls, (b) the purse, and (c) the mushroom." "How, Pop, how do you mean?" "Just think about it." *The One is Unknowable.* They had some kind of lame "ideas day" or something at Bernco State, and a guy at a card-table was pushing Transcendental Meditation, and I made the mistake of getting into an argument with him about why Zen is better. "What a terrible thing to be doing," I realized, after a few minutes. "Arguing brands of enlightenment like station-wagons!" Beige station-wagons. I have a beige station-wagon as well as the '56 Buick. Up here in real time, our Buick is in the shop, Audrey dented it, but I didn't get mad—she thought to tell me after I'd had a big meal. "Taste good, honey?" *The One is Unknowable...* oh who cares, what's the One anyway?

Third teaching. *The One is Right Here.* Can't argue with that. Can you feel it, brother? "Take me now, Lord," is a line my Langhorne College professor friend Hondo Shock told me last year—the operative image is of a tent-meeting, and a guy, like, hanging on the tent-pole in the middle, "Ah know ah been a mizzable sinnah, but now ah'm saved, *take me now sweet Jesus!*" Which is something Hondo would say like when we were walking around in the rain from his house to mine and back, here for weed, there for booze, back and forth, typically on a Thursday night. One time, the best time of all, we were just so high, sitting on a glider on his back porch, both our wives safely asleep, and…it's like we're riding a roller-coaster, rushing through the floppy shapes, the music, and instead of talking words we're synchronizing our brain states just by making noises descriptive of what we might be experiencing, little gabbles and snorks, each sound so *to the point*, the invention of language once again. *The One Is Right Here*—it means you can be as high as you want to, right now, just as you are. High on life. Receiving Truth. The one is right here, baby. Have a nice day.

To go and formulate any "three central teachings of mysticism" violates the second teaching, of course. The finger and the moon. The finger points at the moon, but you have to forget the finger. Why do you *have* to? You don't have to do anything. It's just…you know, have some fun. A really durable lazy-man meditation trick I learned back in grad school was to…pay attention to the spaces between my thoughts. It's like, the time I noticed it, I was walking around the corner to a neighborhood tavern that I was usually scared to go into, me being a hippie and everything. Head-band, man, hair to my shoulders, the mark of Cain on my forehead, the works. And I'd read of this meditation method somewhere, maybe it was in Ram Dass's *Be Here Now*, which I studied assiduously at the time, and found, yes it works, yes, focusing on the head-space in between the conscious thoughts, behind the unspoken words and the zillion opinions. You ever notice how when you look at something familiar you tend to have a quick flash on that object? A received idea, a party-line, like, you know, my desk lamp: *it fell over and broke once, I hope it don't break again.* My typewriter: *I'm glad I got a red one.* A beercan: *good idea to start drinking light beer, too fat anyway.* And so on. All that chatter, but in between there's blank spaces and, in principle, you can put your attention there and expand that zone and feel different than usual. Great technique, and I'm glad every time that I remember to do it. This one time I'm talking about, I got into the feared neighborhood bar, and some old drooler confronts me, "You look like a goddamn Comanche," referring to my rawhide head-band, worn to keep my hair out of my eyes. I give him the big hippie smile and say, "I'm an All-American Boy!" The smile has him reeling, and he says, extending a questioning feeler across the Generation Gap, "Do you like me?" "Sure," I say, deciding to buy a six-pack and leave. "Well, I can't like you," he rails, "till you get a haircut!"

Ah, the hair. I had long hair till last year when, having left teaching for good (I hope) I wanted to modernize, and got the crew-cut. So our dog, his name is Arf—"So smart, our doggie, he can say his own name"—is subject to getting picked up all the time by the dogcatcher. They don't actually use a big net, as far as I can tell, unlike in Duckburg. Arf was a willful puppy, and we had some real problems with him, Man's Best Friend, chew things and shit on the rug, and then he started getting picked up so often that I had to go to court the day after I got my punk haircut, and the Judge had, like, long, blow-dried hair just brushing his polyester collar, with mutton-chop side-burns for sure for sure, and he gets one look at how short my fucking hair is, and doesn't want to hear a word from me. No respect for society, running around with short hair. God, what a non-issue it turned out to be after all, the hair. Just, you know…whatever makes the straights uptight.

Once I had to see a judge back when I still had long hair, this was in the Bernco era, I'd gone to a big Philosophy of Science Conference in some hick burg in Canada. As I mentioned, I had a habit then of shoplifting books from college bookstores, and figured it would be OK up there, too. I was really broke—to the point where instead of renting a room I was sleeping in a ditch next to the university parking lot. Using a sleeping bag at least, but truly sleeping in a ditch, and all night dreaming about being arrested. A premonition. Sure as shit, next day I try to walk out of the bookstore with a nifty title, *Thirty Years of Foundational Studies*, by Andrjez Mostowski. And I get popped, oh Lord, the British-style pig is there in minutes and he drives me to the cop-shop, a precinct lock-up, like, and I'm photographed and fingerprinted and slammed in there for the night. They leave the lights on, right, and have loud easy-listening music playing. As the night wears on, more and more guys get marched in, toothless degenerate winos, by and large, I'm glad to have a single, with my own sink and toilet, the sink cleverly arranged to drain into the toilet, I had one paperback anthology of SF stories I'd paid for, by way of trying to distract from the Mostowski heist. Mostowski himself, curiously enough, had died the day before—I'd come up to Canada hoping to meet him, the Poles, as I mentioned, were always big on my work in the theory of classes and sets. I thought maybe to channel some of M's free-floating soul energy along with his snatched book, but not so. This SF book that I had in my cell, there was one special story in it, a tale by my favorite childhood writer, Robert Sheckley, "The World of Heart's Desire." Great story, about a guy who brings precious stuff to a hidden scientist to get an injection that will take the guy to his world of heart's desire for a year, like, shunt him into to a parallel universe for a whole year of mental time. So he gets the shot and he goes home and there's his family and he has, oh, problems with the house, and his job to do, and the kids growing up, no big deal, then *wham* the shot's worn off and he's back at the weird scientist's cave and, you realize, in fact there is no house and family, no, the actual world in which this took place is a post-WWIII-holocaust world. And his "world of heart's desire" was just his familiar ordinary life, such as I myself once had in Bernco and *now had ruined*, oh God please help me, get me out of jail, I'm ready to freak out, but not nearly as bad as the obnoxious lad two cells down, yelling to me, "Yank? Yank? Got a match?" Passing matches and cigarettes around being a primo occupation in the hoosegow.

Next day it's all winos and me and the young guy, who's in for stealing audio tapes. He proudly shows me he's got three more stolen tapes in his pants that they didn't notice. Handcuff me to him, the cops do, good god, I don't even know this person. He keeps babbling about being "fried," first time I've heard the word used in that sense. "Yeah, Yank, when we get out, you come over to where I rent a room and we'll listen to some REO Speedwagon and get really fried." *Rrright!* So now we're moved to cells in the main jail, where the court is, and some heavy felons are in the mix. The way that no matter how hard you try, you can't get a corpse to wake up? If you're behind case-hardened steel bars, then no matter how hard you try, *you can't get out.* You really really cannot get out. The guy in the cell next to me was a space-case. I couldn't see him, but the guy across the walkway could, and he starts asking my neighbor some questions. "Why do you have the tips of your boots painted green?" "I don't want to talk about it." "Come on, buddy, what's the story, what's the green boots for?" "Well, all right, you've asked twice and I'll tell you. I come from a special place called Star Nine. It's at the edge of the Earth's atmosphere. I have films of Minister Trudeau sucking off Richard Nixon. I'm going to blow things wide open—in good time." I'm starting to laugh here, and I shout, like, "You're nuts." As the guy rants on, I'm feeling pretty safe, as, after all, he's behind bars, and can in no wise get his deranged hands around my throat.

But I should have kept quiet. I kind of realized this after he still kept talking on and on, a torrent of madness we're all listening to, up and down the cell-block, "Look, I'll tell you guys the truth, I'm God. I control the solar system." I kind of hoot there, you know, I'm still speaking up for straight science but—*oh shit*—I'm seeing the solar system. "Yes, I can put it out in the air there," the guy is saying, hypnotizing us maybe, our already beaten-down brains picking up on his vision. Out there in the cell-block corridor is floating a tiny bright ball, the SUN, and little EARTH too, all pearly blue and white, and the MOON—I look away, look back, the orbs are slowly circling, I can't possibly be seeing this, but I am. Then *whanggg* the pigs are there opening up our cells, and I've been making fun of the fucking Master of Space and Time, and here he is right in line ahead of me, definitely a criminal type, my dear, and he shoots me a look that makes me glad the police are there to keep him from ripping out my throat. So each of us gets up in front of the judge with a public defender whom we'd talked to or not, and the Master of Space and Time just…bullshits the judge that he is his own brother and they've picked up the wrong guy, and for a second there everything gets all hazy and confused and the judge apologizes and lets the Master leave. But not so in my case, long-hair/short-hair, you dig, well no big deal, I'm just sentenced to the night that I'd already spent in jail, and I have to pay a fine, and I phone my long-suffering Pop and he wires some money.

Driving home to America I was tense, you bet. I'd called Audrey the night before from jail and—she later tells me—in the flash of my "I'm in jail" message, she'd been sure I was in for murder. Assuming the worst. I wanted to call her on the way back home, so I went into some sleazy Canadian non-chain diner and asked, "Do you have a phone," and the little girl behind the counter looks at me real scared and funny and she backs off, staring at me. She says "I'll see," and disappears into the kitchen. *I'll see?* I mean, shouldn't she know if they have a phone? And then my eye lights on, dig this, a police-artist-composite-sketch of a mad-dog rapist-killer who looks…*uh*, a lot like me: "Has American accent, strong body-odor, long hair…" So I run out of the place, figuring the little girl is calling the cops, and I speed off, making it that much clearer that I *am* the wanted man, the killer, and if they pick me up it'll be "previous criminal record," and, cresting the next hill I look ahead and see… flashing lights. Help me, Jesus! The lights are just from a road-crew, though, and I get back home safe.

This all came down during my period of toying with the idea that I was controlling reality, like by making Jimmy Fly have a flat tire outside the Drop Inn that time. But I lost interest in the controlling-all-reality concept due to my mounting sense that if *did* control reality I'd completely screw it up, and end up like Eddie Machotka when he was running that rap about the cover of *Abbey Road*. I became somehow scared even to think about the underlying One/Many problem of multiple-wizard world-control, although I suppose one should take every possible option seriously—including power over reality. Don Juan—the writer Carlos Castaneda's hero—used to say the man of knowledge has four enemies: fear, clarity, power, and old age. Thereby suggesting that you might indeed reach a psychic state of extreme power. But I was starting to think the Castaneda books might be a shuck, a head-game. Real life isn't a game, year after year. It gets serious. No it doesn't. It it it. What am I even talking about? There are no secrets to life, there's just good stories, patterns in the fog. Of course something must lie beyond it, and sometimes you can feel it, though it's hard to put it into words.

In graduate-school, reading the mystical Ouspensky, and then still reading him at Bernco, I used to think maybe there was some special place to go where they would give me the answers. In Ouspensky's *In Search of the Miraculous*, he repeatedly quotes G. I. Gurdjieff as saying that one needs a "school" to foster spiritual growth. And I would fret about where to find one of these power-center schools, not realizing that really Gurdjieff had been—let's face it—something of a con-man. The guru scam. "Without a school (*my* school, or a franchised affiliate) you're nowhere." In Bernco I did actually hook in with a Gurdjieff group, they met up in Rochester every Thursday night—Thursday somehow being the opposite of Sunday. We met in the Rochester Public Library, and sat in a circle, and one guy read stuff from Ouspensky or Gurdjieff, and then we'd discuss it, chew the fat at it were. One of my fellow-seekers I remember in particular, a guy with a huge, misshapen head, a brow the size of my face, a man of such brain-weight as to be almost a mental defective. One of us would ask the group-leader a question, and *get the stare*. The stare came from a slight, plain woman sitting next to the leader. She was the energy behind the thing, man, I used to ask any old question just to pick up on that hard-radiation zap of her stare. Eye-contact from strangers always a heavy trip.

The only other "mystical school" I went to was the Naropa Institute in Boulder, Colorado, although this time I was sort of a teacher. Naropa was the brain-child of a Tibetan guru who brought his followers there, they called him Rimpoche. I had a math friend who was in the organization, and he got Audrey and me invited out there in the summer of 1981, after my first year of teaching at the Langhorne Woman's College in Killeville. At Naropa, I was to give a series of three or four lectures on the One/Many problem. For me, the big thrill was to meet my beatnik heroes, Allen Ginsberg and William Burroughs, scheduled to talk on writing, also Gregory Corso would show up. "The Jack Kerouac Disembodied School of Poetics," is what they called the whole literary aspect of Naropa.

At Burroughs's seminar, there he is in his coat and tie, bone-dry voice, reading this and that, then answering questions. I'd glimpsed the man before, in Paris when we'd both been invited to speak at some nebulous psychiatry conference. That time, in Paris, Burroughs was talking about *how to keep people from seeing you.* The basic move being to see them first, and by staring at them, to keep them from looking at you. And he'd actually used this trick on me in the Paris hotel, me longing to "have a chat" and then being in the elevator with him, but not noticing him. When we get out of that elevator Audrey asks me, "Didn't you notice who you were standing next to, Rad?" But in Boulder, old Bill was a real sitting duck, right in front of all us arty types, with Allen G. saintly helpful selfless fixing window, mike, chairs. At Q & A time, I ask Burroughs, "Do you have any good SF ideas on how to send yourself into outer space without using rockets?" Burroughs: "Go as a virus. Code your information in a bug which others catch." Me: "You used to say the word is the virus. Now would you say that the artist is reproducing his software in a virus-like fashion so that later readers participate in his consciousness?" Burroughs: "That's why they call us the immortals." Some strange resonance there—every now and then I have a faint feeling like I'm from outer space myself.

My main friend new at Naropa was a Filipino guy called Arturo. He and his wife June taught Tai Chi, which seemed more or less like Indian-wrestling. Arturo was always high, always with a pint of brandy and a pipe of weed, telling Audrey the secret of life: "Life is a river. A long and winding river." I loved it, talking with him was like being with Cheech and Chong rolled into one. I'd complain to him about my worries about getting fucked up too much. Arturo: "What fucked up, is he fucked up, is this cat fucked up?" One night I'm over at Arturo's, loud music haw-haw, streaks and flares, "Let's do a hot-tub," says hostess June. I'm thrilled to bits, out-west hot-tub, but our kids are freaked at any prospect of undressing, and Audrey also not into it. They split and

115

I stay, and start bragging about what a great writer I am, the new Jack Kerouac, June and Arturo dig it, they say, "Well, we'll tell Allen to come over." And then like I turn around and *whammo*, Ginsberg is there, I give him a jay, we get off a little. And I'm trying to tell about high-school Hank and me reading "Howl" aloud to our wondering girlfriends—but Allen's heard that routine a lot of times. His interest picks up when I say I want to write like Jack, and now I beg a boon. "What I want from you, Allen, after being hung-up on the beatniks all these years, what I want is your blessing." And real fast he whaps his hand down on my head like a skull-cap or electric-chair metal cap *zzt zzt* "BLESS YOU!" he yells. We sit down and rap for awhile on the couch, "Why did the beatniks get so much ink?" "Fine writing." Sure, man, and then it's into the hot-tub with Allen and Arturo, also Allen's young boyfriend, passing around some brandy, remembering articles about people drinking and drowning in hot-tubs, yes let's have that too, so I lean down face-down in the bubbles, nod out, the air *bloo bloo blug* bubble float, heated water, no gravity, people tap my back, float, see the wheat field sliding diagonally, the train rushes by, we ride it to Shangri-La, there's a tunnel with sparks, the idol shrinks. Sit up, and a friendly fat woman is next to me. Later, quoting Kerouac haikus with Allen. I recite my favorite, and Allen says Neal liked that one too.

> Useless, useless.
> Heavy rain driving
> into the sea.

Audrey and I took the kids out to the Coors Brewery for a tour, we were excited about getting Audrey earrings that were two tiny Coors cans so cute. "Your old lady, man," says Arturo, looking at them. "Your old lady." Which was a nice way to think of Audrey—not my good angel, or little wifey, but my old lady, Mamma Audrey with beer-can earrings and frizz-bop hair. Lipstick. We had fun out there. One night Allen was reciting poetry with a new-wave band, the Gluons, and Arturo drifts in, sits with us, and it's out with his trusty corncob weed-pipe, "You think they throw me out for this?" I get off right away, jagged and uptight, clubfoot tightrope, mad ambition. "Relax," says Arturo, I come back with, "Sure, relax, but if I relax too much I wouldn't be here or bother to breathe, right?" "Relax!" Which, come to think of it, is what Allen had told me years before, when I'd seen him doing a poetry reading with his father—who wrote pretty weak Ogden-Nash-type ditties—the two of them had read at Rutgers, father & son, and after the reading I'd pressed forward to ask Allen my big question of that particular day: "Do you think dying is like taking acid?" He looks me over, takes in my tension and raps out, "Relax!" Then softens and says, "It's probably easier."

So anyway, at the Boulder nightclub I'm relaxed with Arturo, and Gregory Corso is right there, I'm hoping to pick up some scraps of beat wisdom from him, vicious criminal though he looks like, but first I go out on the floor to dance some with Arturo and Audrey. On the little stairs down to the dance-floor Arturo does a great Tai Chi move—falls down, but in such a way that it's possible to catch him. Then Allen reads his new poem, "Birdbrain," snaking back and forth, bald head twitching, a Hindu dancer, holding up a sheaf of papers, "I am Birdbrain!" And "I declare Birdbrain to be victor in the Poetry Contest!" A break, and I tap Gregory on the shoulder, he whirls around, "Do you so love me?" He pushes his face an inch away from mine, "Do you so love me?" "Uh, yeah, sure." "Why?" "Well, I always really dug Jack and he was your friend…" "OK. We're all here. We're all here but something's wrong. What?" "Jack's dead." "You got it. Lissen to this. *Blukka*. Whatsat mean? Blukka." "I don't know." "Here and now. Like right there,

117

trying to understand that, you got a blukka." "Yeah, sure. Satori." I jerk in excitement and our heads bang hard into each other. "Here and now," says Gregory. "Like you can't hold onto it. Let it go past. A knot on your head." On the stage, Allen is back. "This poem is for Gregory Corso," he says. Gregory, reacting to that, locks his head on my shoulder to continue talking, head to head like prisoners in Attica. I'd seen them do that at the poetry workshop I taught at Attica one time with Jimmy Fly. Two guys, instead of doing the "class" sat knee to knee with their heads on each other's shoulders, mouth to ear, ear to mouth, talking private, planning drug deals, escapes, who knows. In Attica, there were still a lot of bullet holes, chipped out of the walls inside, left over from the big riot when all those guys got killed. Talk about feeling locked up. I read them some of *The Circular Scale*, that being my very first SF novel, which I'd written in Bernco. I read out a prison scene inspired by my tiny Canadian shoplifting bust. One old guy scribbled while I read, some old black murderer, and then he came back at me with an incredible rap-poem about robots and energy bolts. Another guy, a shy young white guy, showed me his notebook full of special pin-ups. *Anyway*, in Boulder with the Gluons, Allen is reading, and Gregory is talking into my ear, still elaborating on his rap. "I knew a guy who died. I knew a guy who died." "You mean Jack?" "I knew him, you know. And he died. I didn't meet him *after* he was dead. *I knew a guy who died.*" "Yeah." I really feel we should be listening to Ginsberg's poem. Gregory chuckles and leans back, picking up on my tension. "Look at him," he says admiringly. "Look at Ginsey go." Ginsey is flickering like a flame, his head dancing and spouting total communist propaganda, it's just so beat. "He's the master," says Gregory. "We're like two guys at a ball-game. On the mound, the master. The master. Two guys in the stands." Then the poem's over and Allen walks back, "Did you listen to your poem, Gregory?" Audrey starts running some rap of her own on Gregory then, and he rolls up his sleeve to reveal his special tattoo. It's a little oval with a red dot and a green dot inside the oval, and coming off the top of the oval is a line which branches at its end. "What is it?" Gregory says to Audrey. "It's a stop-light," comes back my old lady. "No, it's the first thing man ever drew. What you got here is the brush and the bag to keep…what they paint with, the stuff. And the place to dip different colors, the palette. It's the first thing man ever painted. His tools." Outside it was raining and I *drove*, golfstyle, a discarded lime wedge from June's drink with the handle-loop of my umbrella, then faded out with Audrey. A big time.

As I mentioned, I'd glimpsed Burroughs at a strange conference in Paris, 1979, when we were living in Heidelberg, shortly before I came back to the US to teach at Langhorne Woman's College. The conference was a meeting of the so-called International Congress of Psychoanalysis, headed by an antic character called Armando Verdiglione, a short, very oily guy, usually with a cigar, and always yakking, more or less incomprehensibly, no matter which simultaneous translation you listened to. He liked to theorize about "The Mouth," heavy into orality for sure. He'd somehow heard of me while I was at the Mathematics Institute at Heidelberg; he phoned me up there and asked me to come to his Paris con. So Audrey and I went for the weekend, unsure if Verdiglione would pick up our hotel bill or not—I was speaking on something to do with Gödel's Incompleteness Theorem, I think. Man, that was a good trip. The con's overarching topic was…hard for me to discern, because it was such total bullshit from the beginning to end. Even my no doubt closely-reasoned talk came across as whale-shit, especially as I chose to speak in French—and I speak French very badly. All I can remember is that—oh, right, my talk was called "Towards Robot Consciousness." My basic contention was that since even a piece of wood, as I like to say, is conscious, it's no problem to say that a robot is conscious. Eventually a version of that idea made it into my SF novel *Yes and No* about smart robots, and into my non-fiction book about infinity as well. The con-organizer Verdiglione had some impressive women assistants, one of them I remember especially, a Guila who looked like Sophia Loren, over six feet tall in her high heels, she was a psychiatrist in Venice. Later, in Killeville, I'd use my fleeting impressions of Giulia as a model for a Red-Brigade-type terrorist character in my disreputable fourth SF novel, *The Attack of the Giant Ass*. At the conference, I had a lunch with Giulia and some of her girlfriends, all of them Italian and not speaking English. I ordered a steak with french fries and ketchup, the women watching the American eat ketchup, very satisfying for all of us. "What has this conference been about?" I asked them in my halting French, that being our only mutual language. "The teachings of the psychiatrist Lacan." I had never heard of him, and wanted to know what his special angle was. "The short session. Often he sees patients for only five minutes instead of the traditional fifty." The con-man supreme!

The greatest joy in Paris that time for Audrey and me was eating a lot of oysters. Henry Miller writes about eating oysters at the Dôme cafe in the Montparnasse district. Audrey even found the ultimate Henry Miller oyster-rap passage: "On the ocean floor, the oysters are doing the St. Vitus Dance, some with lockjaw, and some with double-jointed knees." Gusto! At midnight, the whole of the Dôme is filled with well-dressed men and ladies, all very gay and animated, and—strangest of all for an American—not dead drunk, but rather, eating food. Eating food at midnight! The couple next to us were a dapper man with a beard and his charming wife, the nicest little Parisian wife imaginable. Audrey and I were having oysters, yes, and there are so many kinds of oysters in Paris that you order (a) by type of oyster, and (b) by size. There are, for example, the type called Belons and the type called Claires, and if you want Claires, you can have size No. 1, No. 2, or Numero 3. And a great dry wine called Muscadet which is not—though it sounds that way—anything like Muscatel. "How can you eat supper so late?" I ask the dapper guy next to us. "For me," he says—and this is the perfect French answer—"For me, eating is a form of self-expression." We four talked some more, and they were nice, although maybe, it began to seem, hoping too hard to come sponge off us in America. "But wait, we live in West Yakshit, North Dakota, man." Charlie Chaplin has a nice leg-move when he's about to leave the scene of some caper, he rocks to one side and holds one leg straight, with his foot a little above the ground, and he waggles that leg like a stick, the whole length of it, as if he's shaking loose a turd stuck inside his trouser leg. In the end, as I'd hoped, Verdiglione picked up the hotel tab for Audrey and me. A happy trip.

We were running out of grant-time in Heidelberg, and in February, 1980, I visited the US for two weeks, scouting for an American teaching job, doing some interviews, including the decisive one at Langhorne Woman's College, At the start of the trip, I had a few extra days when I stayed with Eddie and his wife and baby in NYC. By now Eddie was making a decent living as a cameraman, shooting film and video. I had this one big day with Eddie when we two got high, and I saw a live sex show on 42nd St, very memorable, here we go.

"What do you want to do now, Conrad?"

Eddie and I are standing out on Fifth Avenue. We've just been to see the photos at the Museum of Modern Art. It's a sunny February day. Eddie's the only White Rastafarian in sight. "Let's go downtown and score some dope, Ed." "OK." I'd expected Eddie to have a good stash when I visited him.

But I'd happened in on a trough—and this was before the era of the marijuana stores. I haven't smoked pot for a year. All Eddie has is some poisonous-green home-grown, good for brewing headache tea. Listening to his huge reggae record collection last night, we'd tried smoking some anyway. Better than cigarettes, and my head's still a little...loose. "*Jah-jah be my eyesight.*" Singing that and walking crosstown to the B-way line. It's Burning Spear, he sings with his neck stretched forward like a goose. "*My way is long, for the road is so foggy foggy.*" You can hear the fog in his voice. My road is so foggy. That means the future is uncertain. Time branches. The music is like garbage underfoot. Beautiful garbage, blowing all up and down the streets of NYC.

The graffiti on the subway cars has evolved during the two years I've been in Germany. You can't read the names at all anymore. The wild abstract expressionist "lettering" covers all the windows so you have to just know where to get out. Everyone *does* know, except the junk-sick stick-thin black man shouting, "My number come in," shuddering there with empty seats around him, running his fingers through an astral heap of zero-dollar bills. Blank Eddie hovers there in the fluorescent light like a big, cautious fish. "Muh numbuh come in!" Crash, roar, crash, roar, crash—we're on Fifteenth Street. Down the stairs uptown, up the stairs downtown. Who needs matter-transmitters when you've got subways? Crash-roar and everything's different!

Out there it's still a sunny February day, a cold day, a street of houses. Down the block there's a liveried chauffeur smoking a spliff outside his dark-blue Buick. Secret smiles. "We should try Union Square," Eddie says, "I had to wait for someone there this summer and twenty guys must have come up." "You think they'll be there today?" Eddie: "Are you kidding?" An interracial cordon of smilers greets us. "Pot?" "Powders?" "Black beauties?" It's like the New York Stock Exchange, with futures, pasts and presents. "Let me see it first," I say to a pot dealer. He hands over a tiny manila envelope. Lots of seeds in there, winking up at me. Maybe it's good if there's seeds. It's not oregano. I give him a five-dollar bill and we move on. But now a subproblem: we don't have rolling papers.

Eddie is disdainful of my score. "I'll make some phone-calls," he says and disappears. Then he's back. "My friend Dan says we can come over. He's very busy, but he'll give us a jay. He smokes only the *best*." Eddie says this with absolute conviction, his Paul Newman lips compressed to a line inside his Moses beard. Who needs telepathy if you've got telephones? We walk two blocks...all this motion, from here to there...how is it possible? Dan meets us in the hall. Wet paint. He's a house-painter. "This is Conrad," says Eddie. "He's my favorite science-fiction writer." "Eddie's told me about you," Dan tells me with a smooth smile. He hands Eddie a fat spliff. "This stuff is very...*resinous*. Have a good time with it." I make Eddie light the reefer as soon as we've walked a block.

Two hits and the air has that great clear-gelatin look to it. Communing with space. I can feel the pressure between the buildings, the long trough of the street, the art noveau complexities trailing my hands...not just space, but space-time! The light is clear and yellow. It's a whole different city again, like taking the subway, crash-roar and we're in a... new place. I start trying to explain this to Eddie. He doesn't care. He doesn't not care. He just strides along, his clotted welcome-mat of hair behind him. My mouth is running. "It's parallel worlds, you dig. We rode your elevator to the street, got a subway downtown, walked crosstown. And dope is like moving in a different dimension. The fourth dimension. We didn't move at all in regular space, but now we're in a different place." "In my building, " says Eddie, "Listen to what somebody scratched in the elevator: THIS IS A BOX THAT CANNOT WALK! SO? YOU?" High Eddie laughter.

We cross Avenue A. The blocks are smaller way down here in the East village. It's a good feeling to know that I'm by no means the first person to walk these sidewalks completely zonked. Eddie has his camera along and stops to take a picture of something on a church. I stand there, like a bodyguard in my long black German overcoat, and old people shuffle around us, anxious of sudden gestures. Stoned and loitering, there's a feeling of being on the other side, an alien. Eddie wants to show me a place called Reggae Record Ranch. It's on 7th Street near Avenue B. A storefront with the windows covered. No way I would ever have found it, much less gone in. Good loud Jamaican music in there, highly evolved. A three meter by four meter floor covered with linoleum patterned like a zebra-hide. The light is yellow, gelatinous. A high counter across the back of the room, with a Jamaican behind it talking to two others. They know Eddie. Eddie has just finished a gig as a cameraman on *Rockers*, a reggae movie. He was down in Jamaica, shooting for months. That's when he became a White Rastafarian. I can't understand what anyone's saying at all, but I walk up to the high counter and hold out my hand to the man behind it. He touches my hand. "Garfield." He's wearing a very high-crowned felt hat, sort of a space-dilated derby. It's wooly and a nice pink and gray plaid. There's an X scar on Garfield's nose. I ease back to the wall, leaning against the room's single record rack, keeping an eye on Eddie, feeling like a gunsel. The music in here is really good. There's Garfield behind the counter, and a guy across the room who's clearly a Jamaican musician. He has the dreadlocks, wears about ten rings, and he sports a ROCKERS button. He and I keep making and breaking eye-contact. I've got to say something, just to relieve the pressure. "Who's this record by?" I ask whitely. "Oh this is a round thing some brothers razza jive fa-tazz comin in you say I mean diggin it out the burnin seed in there sha-bazzo wrap in there the burnin seed you gettin got..." There's more, and while he talks, a big stoned grin crawls out of my mouth. He stops and cracks a slight smile. "You know what I'm talking about?" "Well, yes, I mean generally speaking..."

Eddie's been conferring with Garfield all this time. Garfield cuts off the record that's playing...this is Garfield's *disco*, I realize. He puts on...but can't be! He's playing "Memo from Turner!" My all-time favorite Mick Jagger song that I've never heard again since I saw *Performance* in Berkeley these ten years gone. Great film. I still know the words to "Memo," I can still see Jagger, with a light swinging back and forth over his head, and Jagger is dressed like a business-man, leaning across a desk and shaking his finger. I hold my coat out like bat-wings and start dancing. The Rastas watch impassively, more alien than anything any fevered middle-class imagination has ever come up with. The song is over and I ask the musician with the dreadlocks his name. "Richard...but they call me Dirty Harry."

This is a good parallel world we've hit on. Eddie buys me the Jagger record and a pack of Big Bambu rolling paper, and we hit the street. "What's it like in Jamaica, Eddie?" "Like in there, but when you walk out the door you're still inside." We hunker down in a sunny doorway and get out my little thumb-sized envelope of street weed with its seeds and sand and mouse turds...if you really cleaned it, there wouldn't be anything left. We split the stash in two, and each roll ourselves a big, tapering bomber. There's no *rush* in the stuff, but it does touch up that initial spacey high like a coat of fresh paint. We smoke while walking a few blocks, then ditch the butts...*stoned and clean*. Hundreds of Puerto Rican kids are out of school, swarming up and down the short blocks, staring at us. A man cool and muscular as a snake watches us, unblinking, standing in the doorway of the FAMILY SOCIAL CLUB. "I'm getting uptight, Eddie.

Get us out of here." "OK." But there's no subway, no more dope, no matter-transmission, just step after step in the cold wind, weaving down the street like aliens from NGC 38, the kids look at us with open curiosity, *por favor*, ya'll. I wish I was back in Jamaica, man, with three red suns overhead and a methane rainbow... "Let's get a cab, Eddie." He looks at me unbelievingly. Eddie knows every subway station in Manhattan and I want to take a cab? "I'll be happy to *ride* in a cab, Conrad." "Don't worry, I'll pay." Inside the cab it's warm and like a kountry kitchen with brick-patterned vinyl paper glued to the back of the front seat. We get out at Times Square, I pay the cab, and Eddie catches a subway uptown. I'm standing there alone on Broadway, looking around with bright, omnivorous interest.

Right on 42nd Street just east of Broadway is the place I'm looking for, an ex-movie theater with LIVE LOVE SEX on the marquee TWELVE BOY-GIRL SHOWS A DAY. The admission is an utterly reasonable $3.49, and I scuttle on in. The theater is huge, and they're filling in the time between acts with a giant porno movie. Projected to big-screen size, the 16mm images are milky, translucent. I check out my fellow sex-enthusiasts. Except for one young couple, who look like their marriage counselor sent them over from Bayonne NJ, it's all Japanese tourists and sixty-year-old men. And me. And...then *click*, *buzz*, the film stops and a spotlight comes on. There's a bed on the stage, I notice now, it's tilted up about 10 degrees for better viewing and...everyone starts moving up...will I be able to see? The first row is packed as solid as the Steelers defensive line, sixty-year-old men slotted in there shoulder-to-shoulder, *they* know the score. I grab a seat in the second row. The music comes on and the girl steps out on stage. She's...beautiful! A Fifth Avenue model, with the perfect curly hairdo and dark lipstick, cool shades that are dark at the top and light at the bottom...she's wearing a sort of silk swimsuit or teddy or camisole and dancing. This woman is going to fuck and I can watch her! Her face is expressionless, but her slim ass is dimpling at us, she's casual but not too casual, excited but not too excited. One song one tit, two songs both breasts, and then she's naked up there, dancing naked with real pubic hair. I feel like cheering! It's a blow for freedom, it really is. I haven't felt so uplifted since going to see the Stones at the Buffalo stadium, two months before we had to leave the country. Now I'm back at last, and there's live sex! She swivels onto the bed and freezes, sitting on the edge toward us with her feet together and drawn up, her knees spread wide. If she wiggled or smiled now, it would be...too much. But as it is, it's iconic, of higher significance, the real thing!

A guy comes walking down the aisle in a bathrobe. He jumps up on the stage. The male lead! He's a wise-ass hoodlum with John Travolta hair and a smile that won't quit. She's so glad to see him that she takes off her sunglasses. He slips off his robe and gets right down to it. Heavy foreplay. Like exhibition wrestlers, they move smoothly from hold to hold. He's running the show, guiding her around, but it's all fun and love. They kiss and talk when their faces come near each other. They never look at us. We all keep real quiet, and I, for one, am too fascinated to even have a hard-on. Later, when I think about it, I'll be excited, but for now it's a Holy Mystery. A faster song comes on...it's all disco of course...and now he's on top and, all right now, they're doing it. Yes! He's putting it to her, and she's into it, man, the old in-out, they're bouncing that slanting bed, her high-heels are digging into his back... Time for the climax! A baby spotlight focuses on him. He whips out his huge distended pecker and...he's spurting! The guy is coming, you can see the clotted-arc shadows on his belly...there's no doubt about it! A sigh of relief goes up, even from the Japanese. We're all in this together.

What a relief to participate in something so natural and

decent in this twisted world. The equipment still works. I feel like I'm in church, a little boy again, that old sex-is-god groove. The performers kiss, and it's all over. He stands there, smiling his wise-ass smile. *Stud.* We're all clapping for him, even the girl on the bed, clapping daintily with a pleasant smile. A sudden pang seizes my heart. Is this primal couple going to just *leave*? Are Mommy and Daddy going to leave me 'cause I saw them making babies? Just walk backstage and out of my life...after all we've shared? Not yet! He puts on his robe, a dark-blue karate robe like *I* have, heh, and she wraps herself in the sheet. There is no backstage here at LIVE LOVE SEX, they use the projection booth for dressing, it looks like, which means that the star couple, the Mommy and Daddy, are going to walk right past us, right up the movie theater aisle like anyone else! People are lurching to their feet, stumbling out towards the aisle trying to, got to, want to, get a little...closer. I get out in the aisle too late. There's a flying wedge of sixty-year-old men between me and the BOY-GIRL, so I give up the chase. I know when I'm outclassed.

On the street it's still light, still New York. There's a curious billboard over Times Square, a big round-the-corner Alex Katz mural up there. No writing on it, just pictures of women's faces. Intelligent self-possessed faces, beautiful with Inner Light. Someone's idea of equal time, I guess, the heads up there and the bods down here...but the Inner Light is everywhere today, clear White Light. I buy two loose joints in the subway station and get the train up to Eddie's.

So that's my report on my big day with Eddie. I read an earlier version of it at a second flaky Armando Verdiglione International Congress of Psychoanalysis conference, "Sex and Language," held in New York in 1981, with Eddie on hand to tape my reading with a Sony helical-scan video recorder. The high point of my performance was when I whipped out a squeeze-bulb bicycle horn and honked it to dramatize the moment when the guy comes. This time, Verdiglione didn't pay for my hotel.

But let's get back the job-hunting aspect of my 1980 reconnaissance foray to the U.S. . It felt a little unbelievable to be returning to the same lame struggle for a nest in academe. Like a recurrent nightmare. As usual, I didn't seem to be getting much response with my endless job letters—but I *had* lined up a few prospects. Going for a long-shot, I started by giving a talk on mathematical logic at an IBM academic research center near New York City. I wore a suit, since I figured those guys all would, but they were in jeans and sweaters. "You're trying to look like you work for IBM," they said, laughing. "And we're trying to look like we're professors." They were good guys, but, no, they weren't going to hire me. And then I hit a college in Maryland, and that didn't go over too well. I didn't like them. And then I went to Langhorne Woman's College in Killeville, Virginia, and they seemed to enjoy my talk, I drew a good crowd, and I liked how sunny it was down there. I'd even had a precognitive dream of getting a job at a place with a platypus and, sure enough, the Langhorne lecture hall had a stuffed platypus in a display case. The math chair and I weren't very comfortable with each other, but I had the feeling Langhorne was running out of options, just like me. So it seemed like a done deal. And now, for a final, backup slot, I was supposed to visit a college even further north than Bernco had been. These guys had all but said their job would be mine if only I'd appear for an interview. I was on my way there, at an airport in Syracuse, New York, and it was snowing. Reality check. Snow? "I am *not* going to do this." I said to myself. "No matter what, I am not going to move to where the weather's worse than Bernco." I walked across the lobby and got the next flight back to NYC, spending an extra day with Eddie. This was one of the very few times in my life when I had a definite feeling of exercising free will. Most of the other choices I've made were forced by circumstances, or were a path of least resistance. Nothing was ever so clear-cut as walking across that Syracuse airport lobby. So in the end, it was only Langhorne College that offered me a job—and even that offer was slow to come. The other profs had to pressure the math chairman into hiring me. He and I were like a dog and a cat. Me the dog.

But wait, I still haven't told you much about Heidelberg. I loved the huge old castle hovering above the town like a hallucination. The woods, the food, the fluffy clouds in the pale-blue sky. Downtown they had a shopping street that went three kilometers, all cobblestones, all pedestrians-only, all lovely, lovely shops, the gimcrack-hawkers at one end, the fabulous department stores at the other end, a bit like a street in a theme park and therefore slightly dreadful, but also the best of its kind, a German-solid Platonic archetype of "the street of many shops." We loved a toy-store & stationer's called Knoblauch. Knoblauch was five stories high, counting the basement. In the basement were art supplies, lovely fat German options. The ground floor had wrapping paper and cards and stickers and lots of string, also fancy ribbons with, like, a Smurf every six cm. In Germany a "Smurf" is called a "*Schlumpf.*" We even saw a lithograph of two Schlumpfs *doing* it, although this was at an art show and not at Knoblauch. Running along the staircase up to Knoblauch's second floor they had a sliding-board made of polished wood, it was there just for fun, and to hell with public safety. Public safety is concrete blocks painted lime-green, right? On the second floor of Knoblauch were the toys, Lego sets in particular. Ah, the Lego trips we took, my three kids and I. We were acquiring the little blocks at a great rate. The grandparents had all been giving them to us for a number of years, and we brought about ten pounds of Legos with us to Germany, and while we were over there, Audrey's parents in Geneva were giving us a lot more. Germany didn't have much in the way of kiddie-TV shows, and our kids and their friends did Legos to pass the time, heavily into them, with me also doing Legos more than ever before. We had a period of wild experimentation. Cars out the yin-yang, planes, tie-fighters, shit-bugs, Chinese racer, variations on the wheel. Three special high-points come to mind:

(1) A monolithic solid-Lego man, a huge robotic figure with two yellow legs, a blue torso, a head, etc. He stood about 80 cm high, well, maybe 60 cm. Whatever a cm is.

(2) The "jungles" where the kids and I would labor for hours to make a construction that used every single Lego block we had. Lay out a big base, and then start shooting up stalks, towers, sky-tunnels and bridges above over the busy plastic bumps, stalagmites and stalactites—like three-dimensional static in color: red, yellow, blue, black, and white—that is, the primary colors plus the two amplitude poles.

(3) *The car*! Conrad Jr. and I cannibalized an advanced set that had gears and a chain, then added the motor and battery from our Lego train...everything came in Lego form, even trainsets. After several days of tweaks and invention, our home-brewed car chugged down the guest-house hall, long and low. Little Conrad and I were as proud as the scientists who split the atom. An epic hack.

I got the kids another remarkable toy during our stay, the Elektromann set. "*Alles baut Elektromann, was mann mit Strom betreiben kann.*" "Everything builds Electroman, what one with current energize can." I'd played with a version of this set myself as a 12-year-old pseudo-asthmatic when I was on leave from my German boarding-school and vacationing with my dear old Grandma. Towards the end she liked to sign her letters to me, "Your Uralte

Grandma, 1888." *Uralt* means, like, *primevally old*. Real old. She got me my Elektromann set in 1958, I think it was for Christmas. It came with a great German flat battery with two pieces of metal on the top that if you put them on your tongue (this being Experiment #1 in the Elektromann handbook), you'd get a funny taste of broke-down ions. "*Ei, wie widerlich das schmeckt!*" exclaims the handbook. "Eeek, how repulsive that tastes!" As a boy I worked up through the levels of experiments, five or six a day, wanting to get to the real complex stuff. Finally I built the Bell, a set-up with an electromagnet whose circuit was rhythmically interrupted by a spring on the vibrating clapper so that the bell rings. Fine. Next step after the Bell is to attach an extra wire to the clapper. You take the bell-gong off and use it for a hand-piece, an electrode that the person to get shocked is going to hold. Yes, the Bell becomes Experiment #34, the Electrocuter, with the bell-gong for one hand to hold, and you use the metal-filings-box-become-compass-holder for the other hand. I worked the Electrocuter on my grandmother, "Hold these tight, Grandma." And not only she gets shocked, but she also gets a little stab in her thumb from the tack, which I'd forgotten about, the little tack that you'd balance the compass needle on inside the compass holder. But she thought it was funny. "Oh, you little beast!" she said, in the friendliest way imaginable. Anyway, like I'm saying, in Heidelberg as a grown-up, I bought my Conrad Jr. an Elektromann set at Knoblauch for his birthday. He races through Experiments #1 thru #34, the Electrocuter, and then he extrapolates to—#35! He puts one wire in a basin of water, with a piece of money in the water, and he asks *his* Grandma (my visiting Mom) to hold the compass-needle box and to reach into the water and pick up the coin. Once again, an indulgent shriek. "Conrad! You little beast."

As a boy of 12 or 13, I used to play with a great bunch

of kids outside Grandma's apartment building. This would been when I was on vacation from that Black Forest boarding school. I liked staying with Grandma, although one night, leaving her cozy living room, I saw my bedroom door at some strange angle, and the glass in the top of the door somehow combined with the bedroom window to form a...*shape*, and I screamed. "Auuugh!" "What is it, little beast?" Ah...I couldn't tell her, I thought it was the ghost of my dead grandfather, the original Conrad von Riemann, Grandma's dead husband. My favorite pal in Grandma's neighborhood was Uwe, pronounced *oo-vah*, a strong bright kid whose father ran a fruit stand. I played a game called Balla-Balla with him, a sort of soccer, modified by the constraints of a 5 m x 5 m playing field and a ball like a rubber golfball. They had amazing fireworks in Germany for New Years Eve. Typical German excess, right, all year fireworks are illegal, but for 3 days before Jan 1, you can buy big heavy-duty bombs—Jesus! It was a real *Our Gang* scene out there, countless grubbers like myself roaring around, and my Grandma, after all, not able to do much more than, if it seemed called for, to rap one of her jeweled family rings against the windowpane, her looking down at us from her apartment building's second floor. The afternoon of New Years eve, we're setting off big super bang-tubes, M-200's you might call them, long finger-thick hard cardboard rolls, and at one end is...a giant match-head, strike the bastard on the pavement and throw it. The giantest bomb of all was one that a man gave us after it turned dark, this guy reels off the streetcar from his Franz Kafka Insurance Company office, in an overcoat, "*besoffen*," Uwe tells me, pointing at him, "besotted," and we go up to him, begging a boon, and he's like, "*Pmpf-pmfpf*, well, kids, take this," and he hands us a cube about 4 cm per dimension, tightly wrapped in twine, and inside it is several ounces of high explosive. We set the fucker down right by his apartment

133

building's front door, and he reels inside, someone lights our bomb, one of the big kids, and we run like hell, half a block till it goes off BBLLLAA NNNG, the missing letters at the middle of that explosion noise being *white*, man, just pure white ear pain. All right!

For me fireworks are like marijuana. "Something illegal that Bunger usually has, and you need a match." It's essential that fireworks be illegal, it's part of their appeal. In Louisville, they had a big show of rockets every Fourth, at the Louisville Country Club, you could wander out on the golf course and watch them all alone or, better, with a girl, lying down together on the short nap of a golf-green, staring up into the sky's negative abyss now impregnated by the fire-spurts and colors of flame. Pinwheels are the best of all, somehow, the mandala, the burning eye of sparks on tree or fencepost. Once in Louisville, a wealthy family—the family of my art teacher Lennox—they had my parents and us kids over for fireworks, and they lit off two dozen pinwheels at once—paradise!

I'm thinking about fireworks because, up here in real time, tomorrow's the Fourth of July, 1983. A flag on our porch. I like the idea of encountering the Flag in an individual and subjective way, as a design pattern, or even as a symbol of being a regular American, but please not an uptight fascist. Ronald Reagan in the press today, interviewed by old Ansel Adams, who reports, "It was like talking to a movie actor." Our president is a movie actor, do I care? What a snare and rip-off of personal energy it is to care about the president. What lame bullshit that you should read the news and worry. Worry when you're broke, worry when your lover leaves you. But don't worry when Cuba invades Angola. Iraq invades Iran. Honduras invades El Salvador. Why care?

Back to the narration. For me, the Sixties ended when I left graduate school to be a math teacher at Bernco State

College. Around then, it was 1972, things really seemed heavy. I'd been doing a lot of yoga—there was even a point when I could get both legs behind my head. The position is called "yogic sleep," and with your ass wedged right under your face you look like a woman with big boobs. The apartment Audrey and I were living in was right across the street from the Jewish Community Center, which had big open grounds that had once been a rich man's estate. There was a broken-up old concrete tennis court. I liked to go out there late at night and do some meditating. Sometimes I'd imagine that I'd managed to stop breathing for five whole minutes. Next to the tennis courts was a tree that I could, with some difficulty, climb. I liked to sit up there, barefoot, feasting on the incoming sensations. The grounds were right at the lip of a cliff leading down to the Raritan River, and on the other side was New Brunswick. Sitting up in my tree, the clanks and tweets of New Brunswick would float up to me like a single, complexly articulated sound: the sound of a city. Another special feature of this tree was a hollow spot inside one of the branches. There was a beehive inside this hollow, and if I were up there in the evening, I could see bee after bee come angling in through the setting sun's rays to land at the lip of the knothole that opened into the hive. The bees could feel my love for them, right, and they never tried to sting me. At night, when they were all inside their hive, I'd put my ear to the knothole and listen to their buzzing—a wonderful sound as layered and complex as the sound of New Brunswick from across the river.

One special night I had an important vision in the tree. A fine rain was falling, misting through the branches. I'd been working with two different types of meditation technique: (1) All is One, and (2) Stop the World. The first technique consists of merging more and more into the world around you, so that your feeling of being flows out of your body and soaks into your surroundings. The idea here is to identify

135

"I" not with your body, but with universal existence. The second technique consists of trying not to have thoughts, trying to experience the Void, trying to cease to exist as a separate entity. The first technique is consciousness expansion, the second is contraction. On this one special night, I tried doing both techniques at once. That is to say, I was expanding my awareness to include the bees, the raindrops, the tree branches, New Brunswick, the clouds, the sky, etc. And at the same time, I was trying to shrink down below my body-level, below my cell-level, trying to fall through the cracks between my thoughts. My big flash was a sudden conviction that the two techniques were, in some sense, the same—at least as regards ultimate goals. That is, I had an image of two spheres centered on my head, one sphere expanding indefinitely, and the other sphere contracting indefinitely, and then, *flash-flash*, I gained the conviction that the spheres were actually on a collision course, that they'd meet at some attainable place where zero is the same as infinity, *welcome-welcome*, and Everything is the same as Nothing. A heavenly moment.

Eventually I used this vision as the underlying idea for my first novel, *The Circular Scale*. A guy shrinks and shrinks, way down below the atoms, and he finds our same planet Earth down there. Circular scale! I don't know exactly how I came to the point of being able to write this up as a novel. It was the summer of 1976, I think, during one of the long vacations a teacher gets—at this point I was teaching at Bernco State. I wrote a chapter, and another chapter and another, and then the characters were moving around pretty well. Sometimes when I'm writing a novel, I see the scenes happening in my head, and I hear the characters talk. I write it down, tweaking and replaying the action until it's right. The global part can be hard—that is, getting a reasonably coherent plot. Getting the plot is kind of like designing a maze. When you're planning a book, you have the beginning of the book, and you want some kind of happy or dramatic ending, and the beginning-to-end path shouldn't be too obvious. Up at the place in Maine where Mom and Pop went in the summers, I used to draw mazes on the beach for our kids and my nieces and my nephew, the little ones racing around and squealing, the goal a pile of wet seaweed in the middle. The mazes needed extra branchings, complications that twigged off near the beginning and then circled back in near the end. So when I was drawing my mazes, I'd leave plenty of gaps opening off the main path so that later trails could connect. In terms of writing a novel, this means including a number of unexplained or confusing events near the beginning—events whose meaning even you the author don't yet know. And of course you have to be willing to go back and change things near the start so they fit with what happens later. Like erasing pieces of the maze wall wherever you need. I've learned that making a revision never takes as long as I thought it would. Often it's just a matter of changing a few dozen words.

During our first autumn in Heidelberg in 1978, I remember looking up at some torn, scudding clouds and feeling like we were being blown all over the Earth by the blind winds of fate, no home, no center, no plans for the future. "Life is what happens to you while you're waiting for it to begin," said John Lennon. I'd brought my bike along to Germany with us, and when it wasn't raining, I'd ride from our apartment to the office they'd given me in the Mathematics Institute. As I mentioned earlier, I worked on a novel about infinity all through the first winter there, typewriting it in my sound-insulated room at the Institute. *Mt. LSD 26*. They had rubber strips around all the windows and doors, it was wonderfully peaceful. And, to my joy, the very first publisher to whom I sent *Mt. LSD 26* bought it. Ace Books—the original publisher of William Burroughs's *Junkie*! Not that Ace ever meant to publish anything but clever mass-market books they thought would sell. Old Bill and I just happened to sneak in. Hearing of the Ace sale, a British company—Virgin Books—bought *Mt. LSD 26* as well. Virgin was a company that owned a lot of record stores in England; they were also producing punk and new-wave records. They were a vertical monopoly who'd now decided to move horizontally into books as well as records. Their first list of books included my *Mt. LSD 26* and an album of pictures of Sid Vicious as a boy. Vicious had been the bassman for the Sex Pistols, with Johnny Rotten singing. Rotten and Vicious, what a great pair of names. I was proud to be associated with them however tenuously. Later, Sid would be the idol of the first boy to date our daughter Sorrel.

The way I got in contact with Virgin Books was that I met their SF editor by going to my first-ever science-fiction convention in 1979. It was held in Brighton, a seaside resort not too far from London. I took the train over there from Heidelberg, bringing along a Xerox of my typescript for *Mt. LSD 26*—thinking of my father bringing a table he'd designed to a furniture-maker's convention in Chicago years and years ago. When I went to Brighton, Ace hadn't yet bought my novel, and I was looking to make some contacts. And have some fun. As soon as I got to the hotel where the convention was, I saw a freaky guy in lace-up white boots, and I decided to follow him till he sat down. He found his perch with some other exotic Brits and, as I had hoped, they broke out some dope. Instead of having maryjane and rolling joints, they crumbled a piece of hash, mixed it with tobacco, and rolled that. I got super-high almost right away and started rapping to the guys, real friendly fellas who gave me some of their hash to use as my own discretion. What made it so different from a math conference was that the old guys seemed to welcome new blood. In math, there's so few jobs and it's so much hassle to get them that there's some hostility between the established professors and the new ones trying to break in. An elitist, unfriendly scene. Science fiction seemed different. The successful writers were doing good, interesting work that many people liked to read. They could afford to be generous; they had nothing to lose. The market had enough room for everyone. In the evening there was a party with mostly writers, and I managed to get in. I managed to lay my *Mt. LSD 26* draft on a cool editor from Virgin Books, and I got to hang out with a couple of my favorite writers, Robert Sheckley and Ian Watson, both of them very far-out and friendly. Also at the con I picked up a copy of Philip K. Dick's *A Scanner Darkly*, one of the funniest books I've ever read. Black humor about stoned-out guys losing their raps. Getting onto the train out of Brighton after the con, I was reading *Scanner*, and laughing so hard that I left my suitcase on the platform. I suddenly realized this as the train started to move. Jumped back out in the nick of time.

During our first year in Heidelberg we had a very grand apartment, but we couldn't afford it for the second year. The second year we were living in two rooms for about $400 a month. A bedroom, and a living-room with an efficiency kitchen at one end. We put Ida in a crib in the bedroom even though she was too old for it, put the bigger two kids in bunkbeds, and hung a bedspread from the ceiling so they wouldn't always see their parents in bed together. If Audrey and I wanted to make love, we pretty well had to do it in the living room, even though it lacked a real couch, and the floor was concrete with felt glued to it. There *was* nice wood parquet flooring, but for some German reason they'd mounted the wood floor on the ceiling. You could sit on the concrete floor and look up at it.

The wine and beer were cheap, and good, although at first I didn't like German beer—it's very thick, bitter and filling. You have about four of them and you're (a) full and

(b) drunk, unlike nice watery American beer that you can drink and piss out all night. The joy of pissing. Insane as this sounds, I found a way to get hold of American beer. I'd go to the Heidelberg US Army-base PX and pretend to be a soldier. Wear a parka and tuck my hair up into a knit cap—they didn't check ID. The first case of Budweiser I managed to get—what ecstasy! But eventually I came to accept the heavy German pilsener. Audrey and I had a tape player, and when the kids were asleep, we'd drink and dance. I liked to leap up into the air and kick off from our concrete walls. Eddie Machotka had sent us a lot of reggae tapes, and we'd bought some other tapes in Germany. My favorite two tapes were Jimmy Cliff, *The Harder They Come*, and Elvis Costello, *My Aim Is True*. Oh, and Marley's "No Woman No Cry," with its bittersweet nostalgia for Trenchtown—which we, as exiles, could relate to. It seemed like the Seventies were over, and disco finally dead, and the music getting good again. There was a theater in Heidelberg that showed a reggae movie every Saturday at midnight—we went to a lot of them. Wild-looking German students there, but never smoking dope, just harsh cigarettes. Serious about their pleasure, serious about their terrorism.

I had to go down to City Hall every so often and get our visas renewed. They had three offices in the passport division: (1) US and Japan, (2) Greece and Turkey, (3) Other. The Good, the Bad, and the Ugly. You had to wait all day with all kinds of weird guest-workers and guys from the US Army base. I had a moment of satori there one day, I was about to start being uptight about the wasted time, the bureaucracy, the alienation—but somehow I relaxed through it, or past it, under it anyhow, and I saw the hall get clear and calm, and everyone there was a beautiful eye of God. Me sitting there smiling. "No, you go first." Type B behavior. On the wall at City Hall, they had a big poster with pictures of students who were *Gesuchte Terroristen*, meaning *Hunted Terrorists*, about fifty of them, all with good solid German names like Karl-Heinz or Ute, all students who'd done things like shoot a bazooka at an American General's car or rob six banks. They don't fuck around, these German radicals, they don't go sticking flowers in a soldier's gun. Sometimes the police would set up road blocks, also not fucking around, and you'd have to fish out your papers while some guy held a machine-gun aimed at your head. They deserved each other, the police and the terrorists, two sides of the same coin, angels and devils, Mods and Rockers, Jerry Falwell and me.

When Elvis Costello came to play Mannheim, just a half hour from Heidelberg, Audrey and I drove up to see him. Elvis was good, we were right up close to him, so close you could see all the sweat pouring off him. Between songs he'd go backstage and watch a televised British soccer game. His guitarist made faces like a chimpanzee eating a cigarette butt. For some reason, only about two hundred people showed up for the concert, some German punks with black lipstick and green dye in their hair, also some GIs, but mainly just average well-dressed students and shopgirls. Lots of Germans wear black lipstick all through the Karnival season before Lent. Speaking of holidays, before we'd moved, the kids asked me if there's Halloween in Germany, and I'd told them, sweetening my voice, "*Every* day is Halloween in Germany." They knew I was teasing them, and they shouted me down.

My father came to visit us in Germany after we'd been there a year. He'd just gotten divorced from my mother. First he had open-heart surgery—a bypass—and then he flipped out and got the divorce, had more heart trouble then, started taking some strong medicine, and was drinking a lot. Very fat, very out of it. "What day of the week is it?" he'd ask me each morning. "Where am I?" The woman whom Pop had left my mother for came to Heidelberg to meet up

141

with him, and then they went off to Paris. Trying to have fun. I sat there in the train station crying for a long time. "I want my daddy. Who's going to take care of me?" Death and age. We went to see my grandmother a few times in Germany—I'd always liked her a lot. I think the real reason I found it easy to talk to Kurt Gödel at Princeton was that he reminded me so much of Grandma. I saw her a few weeks before she died, at age 91. That last time she looked, when not talking, so very tired and sad. She was almost done. But still—and this kept her going throughout her long life—she was always ready to get interested in anything that might come up: a discussion of what goldfish do in the winter, say, or the preparation of scrambled eggs. She sent me across the street to get eggs while I was there for that last visit, and she cautioned me a dozen times to look both ways crossing the street, as it had a lot of traffic that went fast. Once a baby, always a baby. If, for your parents, you're eternally a teenager, then for your grandparents you're always a grade-school kid.

During our final months in Heidelberg, we hung around a lot with a Hungarian refugee who worked making artificial teeth. His name was Huba. He had a nice German wife and a daughter in Ida's kindergarten—we were making local friends via the kids' schools. If it was sunny, I'd go down to kindergarten to pick up the children and they'd all be running around naked in the playground. Everyone seemed to think that was fine—a less Puritan concept of body-shame in Germany. At a swimming pool I'd often see women *whip* off all their clothes to change into their bathing suit, then later *whip* off the suit off to get dressed again. Whew! All the kindergarten mothers were so well-dressed and nicely groomed. The Germans seemed to have more money than they knew what to do with. Compared to them, Audrey and I were guest-workers.

One of the last nights in Heidelberg, we two stayed up

late drinking bottles of white wine, so late that the sky was getting light. Nearly dawn. Audrey went to bed, and I took yet another bottle of wine outside with our little tape player. Listening to Bob Dylan's *Live at Budokan*. I walked down the long hill to the Neckar River, set the bottle and the tape player on the dock, and swam out into the flow. Death wish? It was gray with the sun coming up, the water metallic and oily, me naked in it, swimming out to touch a passing barge. I survived my folly and headed back up to the large grounds around our apartment building, hearing the birds start up. The birds—god, that noise got in my head, and I couldn't get it out for days, all that tweet-twitter in there with the headache and hangover and my fear of the future.

I did manage to take acid in Germany, my third time ever, Sta-Hi mailed it to me, a black five-pointed star printed on a piece of blotting paper. *Black-star*, he called it on the audio tape cassette he sent me with it, a crazy tape he'd made of whores and dopers in the taxi he was driving out in San Jose, California. I took the acid in my office at the Mathematics Institute, and then, waiting for it to take effect, went out to stroll among some of the University's greenhouses and ornamental shrubs. Looking at a strange-looking tree, at how all its branches spread out, thinking, "Well, yes, now that I've reached a certain level of maturity, there's no reason I can't take a psychedelic substance and just quietly enjoy it…" Seized with stomach cramps then, I hurry back to the Institute to take a shit, but the turd is only one inch long, and floating there mockingly. "Well, there goes my brain," I say, almost gaily, and flush it down. With a 7 km bike ride back to the apartment ahead of me. Near the river I laid down to concentrate, hoping to line up my mindsights and get a zap of White Light. But the air felt like corn oil, and a dog came to lick my face—*uugh*. Riding my bike over the bridge I wondered how it would be to jump off: too much paperwork. Later that year some guy threw his wife off that bridge, and the police made him go back there and re-enact the crime with a big dummy of a woman…so they'd have a picture for the paper, I guess. Laboring up the last hill to our apartment, that Black-Star day, I was sweating and shaking and trying to tuck my shirt in, fumbling at my belt, when here comes a woman walking down the hill, her face a mask of fear and loathing, she thinks I'm going to expose myself, oh Lord. Finally I made it home and told Audrey where I was at, and she was nice to me, and put me in front of the TV with the kids. Later I carried my son outside in his pajamas and we looked at the moon together. "Maybe you'll get to fly there someday," I told him, thinking it was true, my heart bursting.

Then, *whammo*, we were back in the US. We bought a car and a house in like a week. It was so strange to come back, all the bigness still here, the supermarkets! Outside a Winn-Dixie in our just-bought second-hand beige station-wagon, Audrey and I had a moment of ecstasy, with the Beatles "Back in the USSR" on the radio. There's a lot of land not doing anything in particular in the US. In Europe, every square meter is being put to some use. You never see just raw scuzzy woods. Moving to Killeville, Virginia, and seeing woods like that, I kept thinking that there must be tidy walking paths. But a lot of the Virginia woods are inaccessible—thorns and thickets and poison ivy—blank space. People seemed to dress very strangely in Killeville. Like women in lime-green skirts and hot-pink blouses. "Preppy," Sorrel told us this was called. "The preppy look." We couldn't decide if it was a time-warp or a space-warp, that is, whether people looked like this everywhere in America in 1980, or whether they had always looked this way in Killeville. I guess it was a little of both. Pop came to visit us and slept on our living-room couch, on his own, still drinking a lot, but comforting to have around. "I always know what people will say," he told me. Not sounding happy about that. Pop no longer such a central figure in my life—no, it was my time to be the man, the father with growing children, the son with aging parents on their way out.

Most of the students at the Langhorne Woman's College seemed to have Add-A-Bead necklaces, with a few more gold beads appearing on the chains after each holiday with their parents. Mind-numbing conformism. As I've mentioned, the math department chair was a humorless guy, a natural enemy. He had wattles. I came to think of him as "The Suckling Pig." I'd only been teaching there about three months when he told me he wanted to fire me. "Why?" I begged. "You haven't been collecting homework," he says. Me: "I'll collect homework, I will, I promise." "It's not enough just to *do* it, Conrad. You have to *want* to do it." I pretended to want to, and managed to keep the job for one more year only, and then they cut me loose. Despairing of finding another teaching job, and dreading the upheaval of another move, I decided to give freelancing a try. My writing career was in gear. Maybe I could amp it up and make a living.

I rented an office in downtown Killeville to make it official, and Audrey helped me move stuff into it. We'd been having some problems, but things were starting to get better. Here's a poem from my word hoard, it describes that time, "The New Office."

> boxes of books and papers packed
> unpacked left alone
> she helps me, making it
> clean as home, the
> changing home we move
> across the face of the
> Earth scrubbing it
> With eyes and hands no

place for the Bungers or
any place at all really,
just so's I can plug in my
machine, my heart, my
home center that Audrey
and I pass back and
forth like a glass of
water, carried all over
earth, still full.

I began going into my office just about every weekday,
writing, and managing to sell, during my first year, two
books—an all-new pop science volume on the fourth dimension for Houghton Mifflin, plus a cheerful two-mad-sci-
entists novel called *Three Wishes*. And now that first year's
over, and up here in real time I'm typing lies and memories
onto a continuous roll of copier paper that I got at Leech &
Hicks Office Supplies just over the Killeville hill from my
office here, it's a brisk walk through negro streets of dawn
in search of an angry fix, and I have a credit account there,
I'm a real downtown Killeville entrepreneur you bet, the
deal with this roll being that if a copier has a "Select" switch
to choose between letter size or legal size, that means its
paper has to be in a giant roll like paper towels, like the
paper for a teletype machine or for a misty scroll painting,
paper such as the divine Jack K. used for initial mindblast
sevenday draft of *On the Road*, you wave, exactly like that
paper, and I've got it rigged here in back of my dear rose-
red old axe, my IBM Selectric, the paper comes wrapped
around a stout cardboard tube, so I put a sawed-off length of
broom handle through the roll to be a spindle, and I have the
ends of the broom handle propped up on cobbled-together
either-end stands behind my machine, and the ROLL is
threaded though my typewriter and I can type as fast and
hard as I can, and I'm rolling the emergent typed-upon

paper onto a secondary length of cardboard tube that I found in the ruined abandoned building that I rent, and I never have to change the paper, and you were right, so right, dear Jack, my flowing jazz choruses are unbroken by any subliminal beats from turd-counting page breaks...and the only way to gauge the size of this unrevisable mofo is to unroll it and physically measure it...and when I carry it home for safe-keeping each night, I take the black rubber platen roller out from my typewriter to get my SCROLL loose, me goofed gone scribbler scribe, I've got seventy or eighty feet now, and soon, soon, I will butcher it into pages and mail them to editor Gerard at Houghton Mifflin and he will send it back immediately, although I won't realize this for a week, cuz puppy Arf will drag the packet off the front porch into the side yard, there to chew it and roll in it and leave it there to be stumbled upon by me days later, a rainstained object of horror to the gods...*All the Visions.*

Take 3.

So what's the point? I mean, it ought to add up to something, shouldn't it? A guy telling his life story, at length, but it doesn't really come to anything. Well…I guess I would have been glad to read it, glad to see the footprints in the sands of time, yes, glad to know there was once someone vaguely like me, and will be again, no doubt, we are a hive, us humans, no individual death really matters, like when we were at the beach last year and Conrad Jr. caught a lot of crabs—crabs are so stupid that all you do is lower a fish-head or chicken-neck down in the water and the crab grabs it and won't let go and you pull up the string and net him and put him in a bucket with the other crabs you caught, unless you haven't caught any crabs yet, in which case the bucket is empty—and we cooked them for supper, they screamed when I threw them into the boiling water, but screamed so high that it was hard to hear, but not quite so high a scream as lobsters do, we cooked the crabs for supper and poor Conrad started crying, because, you understand, these crabs and him had been out on the dock for several hours, doing a *number* together, biped catching crustacean, and now the poor crabs were dead, but the consoling factor was that, after all, there are still a whole lot more crabs in the ocean, the race of crab not one whit diminished by these individual deaths, no man is an island, if you think of it the right way, "no man is an island," means that in fact an individual death doesn't matter, it's the whole thing, the gestalt that matters, so that, as old Bill suggests, our best way for space colonization would be to send out probes full of bacteria or viruses, just so they have that buddy-buddy double-strand of DNA, ribonucleic acid, the genes, if you think about it, the genes are sitting down deep in us—we are in fact big space probes for the genes, we are meat robots that the genes build in order to reproduce themselves, the other form of immortality being, yeah, software backups, but the final is the realization that even these stabs at immortality are relative, try like 10-to-the-30th years from now, man, when most of the protons have broke down, or 10-to-the-100th years away, and, really if you think about it, what the fuck difference would it make if the world lasted forever, and would it even matter if you yourself didn't have to die, oh, it would get too old, but still, something in one's soul does kind of leap up at the thought of immortality, but it's a con, we have to learn not to fall for it, not get sucked in, because mortality is an essential part of the human condition, like in *Gravity's Rainbow*, Pynchon writes about the angels looking down, "all unaware of the dark beauty of the death-sentence we labor under," the dark beauty, take me now Jesus, well, give me 35 more years, I wanna be 72 when I croak, six feet, a year of six-year months, let's finally get it right, out with the calculator I bought to teach Calculus with, if a year is 72, then 37 is the fifth of July, though today is the eighth, close enough, up here in real time real time real time, *auughh*, it's not real for you anymore, my time, or for me, it's ripped back from me by the current, the flow, I'm going to die, oh so what, who cares, it'll be a relief for sure for sure, though there's no rush is there , but still…as I thought once, "Death is

149

the only thing that makes life bearable," I mean how awful it would be to stand forever on a cloud, with a stiff white hard-on, strumming it, listening to hymns, nasty God walking past to piss on the floor, a chance of a peek up the bluesky folds of Mary's skirt to her silken thighs more whiter than a harp of gold, strum it Jesus, there must be some way out of here, I'm a desperate man, but why bother to be desperate, why do anything when you can groove, though grooving gets so boring, well, not boring, really, it's the hangovers and the stoneover dissociation that's hard to take, year after year, "And do your folks say you are a stranger / do your friends think you be too weird / it's hard to learn to live with so much danger, bay-bih / year after year after year after year," psycho rant stifflegged dead pig axe cross the stage, making everyone feel better they aren't up there, scraping it right down to the rind, what's the point, what's the fucking point, man, why are you alive, why is there something instead of nothing, what's the answer, "The answer," sez Wittgenstein, "is experienced as the vanishing of the questions," *right*, I kin dig it, but hey, the questions come back don't they, you have to come down and make some money, baby, the questions come back later, you get the answer fine, you fall asleep, you lose it, lose it totally, gag me with a chain-saw, baby, lose it totally and then start scratching your head, showering lice-eggs across the schizo-scenario and wondering why be working so hard just to get a stiff dick soft, get a stomach full, horrible animal functions, the way that if you really really have to take a shit you can't think of anything else, just kind of crab-scuttle around, do the limbo under the pay-toilet door, find a guy already in there, flub-gubba-geep, go on outside and "lay your load upon the road / when toilets weren't invented," all this hassle to keep the system at maintenance level, putting bug spray on yourself, all the work to keep your hair oiled and your butt clean and your fillings in, your

socks up, your wounds disinfected and bandaged, your
eyesight corrected, your hearing amplified, your behavior
modified, reformed-alcoholic radio-evangelist republi-
can-congressman, *yes!*—your fungus damped, your itch
scratched, and the piece of food picked out between those
two dancey molars, the brain amused with TV paper book
magazine drug cigarette booze coffee frisco-speedball
organ-music-piped-in-from-the-catacombs-of-Thoth, the
frisson, my dear, "Give us this day our daily rush, on the
nod as thou art in Heaven," in heaven, oh man we are in
heaven for sure for sure…or maybe it'd be better to be in
Hell and limp, instead of forever in Heaven with your
tremendous aching stiff golden erection you guys, or
glowing gold lovely halo you gals, with God's horrible
bunion feet the size of mountains and you're in fact standing
on them though you don't realize it, just singing, and feeling
the better for it, soothing the itch the flaw the egg the
lurking scream the origin of the species, the way Brits are
supposed to always say "D" instead of "R," *The Gdeat
Pydamids*, those guys thought they had something going,
one would imagine, those Egyptians mounding up those
rocks and sand, *Chariots of the Gods?????????* naw, the power
of the weak, *what man can do*, Izzy Tuskman used to yell
at me, "What man can *do*," is, uh, turn other men on, like,
"Take this my body which is given for you," do you think
I'll go to hell for writing that? Oh what's the point, can't
somebody tell me please, not that I'd listen, I've got it all
figured out, I tell you, I know the answer and it's "Sometimes
I feel so happy / sometimes I feel so blue," I mean *surf* it,
bro, hang ten, ho-dad, slide in and out of the reckless wash
of snit-snit bubbles, each a galaxy in itself, and what can
we ever know of the fish who swim below, just be there,
why why, just do this, do that, as a good "bad-attitude"
attitude keep in mind that if enough people believe anything
it's probably wrong, eternally subject to revision, the idea

in history, though each time you figure it out you still have to go to sleep and again wake up and again start over—a day is such a very long time, why would anyone want to live forever, *throb*, the Muse sitting on his face and…*throb*, he's up again, out of bed, around the bend agin, over and over, until, if you're lucky as John Lennon, some mushroom from West Yakshit blows you away, or if you're lucky as Aldous Huxley, your wife shoots you up with acid, meanwhile JFK croaking on TV in the nurses' room, and your old lady's like shooting you up every time your stroke-twitched big wise forever-talking mouth tries to move, uh uh uh, "yes dear, take another hit of chemicals…and fucking *die*, man, and shut up," *into the light now darling, into the light, go now, go peacefully into the light.*